The Maiden Tribute of Modern Babylon

WILLIAM THOMA STEAD

Published in 1885

TABLE OF CONTENTS

PART I. THE MAIDEN TRIBUTE OF MODERN BABYLON

(July 6)

In ancient times, if we may believe the myths of Hellas, Athens, after a disastrous campaign, was compelled by her conqueror to send once every nine years a tribute to Crete of seven youths and seven maidens. The doomed fourteen, who were selected by lot amid the lamentations of the citizens, returned no more. The vessel that bore them to Crete unfurled black sails as the symbol of despair, and on arrival her passengers were flung into the famous Labyrinth of Daedalus, there to wander about blindly until such time as they were devoured by the Minotaur, a frightful monster, half man, half bull, the foul product of an unnatural lust.

"The labyrinth was as large as a town and had countless courts and galleries. Those who entered it could never find their way out again. If they hurried from one to another of the numberless rooms looking for the entrance door, it was all in vain. They only became more hopelessly lost in the bewildering labyrinth, until at last they were devoured by the Minotaur." Twice at each ninth year the Athenians paid the maiden tribute to King Minos, lamenting sorely the dire necessity of bowing to his iron law. When the third tribute came to be exacted, the distress of the city of the Violet Crown was insupportable. From the King's palace to the peasant's hamlet, everywhere were heard cries and groans and the choking sob of despair, until the whole air seemed to vibrate with the sorrow of an unutterable anguish. Then it was that the hero Theseus volunteered to be offered up among those who drew the black balls from the brazen urn of destiny, and

5

the story of his self-sacrifice, his victory, and his triumphant return, is among the most familiar of the tales which since the childhood of the world have kindled the imagination and fired the heart of the human race.

The labyrinth was cunningly wrought like a house; says Ovid, with many rooms and winding passages, that so the shameful creature of lust whose abode it was to be should be far removed from sight.

Destinat hunc Minos thalamis removere pudorem, Multiplicique domo, caecisque includere tectis. Daedalus ingenio fabra celeberrimus artis Ponit opus: turbatque notas, et lumina flexura Ducit in errorera variarum ambage viarum.

And what happened to the victims—the young men and maidens—who were there interned, no one could surely tell. Some say that they were done to death; others that they lived in servile employments to old age. But in this alone do all the stories agree, that those who were once caught in the coils could never retrace their steps, so "inextricable" were the paths, so "blind" the footsteps, so "innumerable" the ways of wrong-doing. On the southern wall of the porch of the cathedral at Lucca there is a slightly traced piece of sculpture, representing the Cretan labyrinth, "out of which," says the legend written in straggling letters at the side, "nobody could get who was inside":—

Hie quern credicus edit Dedalus est laberinthus De quo nullus vadere quirit qui fuit intus.

The fact that the Athenians should have taken so bitterly to heart the paltry maiden tribute that once in nine years they had to pay to the Minotaur seems incredible, almost inconceivable. This very night in London, and every night, year in and year out, not seven maidens only, but many times seven, selected almost as much by chance as those who in the Athenian market-place drew lots as to which should be flung into the Cretan labyrinth, will be offered up as the Maiden Tribute of Modern Babylon. Maidens they were when this morning dawned, but to-night their ruin will be accomplished, and to-morrow they will find themselves within the portals of the maze of London brotheldom. Within that labyrinth wander, like lost souls, the vast host of London prostitutes, whose numbers no man can compute, but who are probably not much below 50,000 strong. Many, no doubt, who venture but a little way within the maze make their escape. But multitudes are swept irresistibly on and on to be destroyed in due season, to give place to others, who also will share their doom.

The maw of the London Minotaur is insatiable, and none that go into the secret recesses of his lair return again. After some years' dolorous wandering in this palace of despair—for "hope of rest to solace there is none, nor e'en of milder pang," save the poisonous anodyne of drink—most of those ensnared to-night will perish, some of them in horrible torture. Yet, so far from this great city being convulsed with woe, London cares for none of these things, and the cultured man of the world, the heir of all the ages, the ultimate product of a long series of civilizations and religions, will shrug his shoulders in scorn at the folly of any one who ventures in public print to raise even the mildest protest against a horror a thousand times more horrible than that which, in the youth of the world, haunted like a nightmare the imagination of mankind. Nevertheless, I have not yet lost faith in the heart and conscience of the English folk, the sturdy innate chivalry and right thinking of our common people; and although I am no vain dreamer of Utopias peopled solely by Sir Galahads and vestal virgins, I am not without hope that there may be some check placed upon this vast tribute of maidens, unwitting or unwilling, which is nightly levied in London by the vices of the rich upon the necessities of the poor.

London's lust annually uses up many thousands of women, who are literally killed and made away with—living sacrifices slain in the service of vice. That may be inevitable, and with that I have nothing to do. But I do ask that those doomed to the house of evil fame shall not be trapped into it unwillingly, and that none shall be beguiled into the chamber of death before they are of an age to read the inscription above the portal—"All hope abandon ye who enter here." If the daughters of the people must be served up as dainty morsels to minister to the passions of the rich, let them at least attain an age when they can understand the nature of the sacrifice which they are asked to make. And if we must cast maidens—not seven, but seven times seven— nightly into the jaws of vice, let us at least see to it that they assent to their own immolation, and are not unwilling sacrifices procured by force and fraud.

That is surely not too much to ask from the dissolute rich. Even considerations of self-interest might lead our rulers to assent to so modest a demand. For the hour of Democracy has struck, and there is no wrong which a man resents like this. If it has not been resented hitherto, it is not because it was not felt. The Roman Republic was founded by the rape of Lucrece, but Lucrece was a member of one of the governing families. A similar offence placed Spain under the domination of the Moors, but there again the victim of Royal licence was the daughter of a Count. But the fathers and brothers whose daughters and sisters are purchased like slaves, not for labour, but for lust, are now at last enrolled among the governing classes—a circumstance full of hope for the nation, but by no means without menace for a class. Many of the French Revolutionists were dissolute enough, but nothing gave such an edge to the guillotine as the memory of the Pare aux Cerfs; and even in our time the horrors that attended the suppression of the Commune were largely due to the despair of the femme vengeresse. Hence, unless the levying of the maiden-tribute in London is shorn of its worst abuses—at present, as I shall show, flourishing unchecked—resentment, which might be appeased by reform, may hereafter be the virus of a social revolution. It is the one explosive which is strong enough to wreck the Throne.

LIBERTY FOR VICE, REPRESSION FOR CRIME

To avoid all misapprehension as to the object with which I propose to set forth the ghastly and criminal features of this infernal traffic, I wish to say emphatically at the outset that, however strongly I may feel as to the imperative importance of morality and chastity, I do not ask for any police interference with the liberty of vice. I ask only for the repression of crime. Sexual immorality, however evil it may be in itself or in its consequences, must be dealt with not by the policeman but by the teacher, so long as the persons contracting are of full age, are perfectly free agents, and in their sin are guilty of no outrage on public morals. Let us by all means apply the sacred principles of free trade to trade in vice, and regulate the relations of the sexes by the higgling of the market and the liberty of private contract. Whatever may be my belief as to the reality and the importance of a transcendental theory of purity in the relations between man and woman, that is an affair for the moralist, not for the legislator.

So far from demanding any increased power for the police, I would rather incline to say to the police, "Hands off," when they interfere arbitrarily with the ordinary operations of the market of vice. But the more freely we permit to adults absolute liberty to dispose of their persons in accordance with the principles of private contract and free trade, the more stringent must be our precautions against the innumerable crimes which spring from vice, as vice itself springs from the impure imaginings of the heart of man. These crimes flourish on every side, unnoticed and unchecked—if, indeed, they are not absolutely encouraged by the law, as they are certainly practised by some legislators and winked at by many administrators of the law. To extirpate vice by Act of Parliament is impossible; but because we must leave vice free that is no reason why we should acquiesce helplessly in the perpetration of crime. And that crime of the most ruthless and abominable description is constantly and systematically practised in London without let or hindrance, I am in a position to prove from my own personal knowledge—a knowledge purchased at a cost of which I prefer not to speak. Those crimes may be roughly classified as follows:—

I. The sale and purchase and violation of children. II. The procuration of virgins. III. The entrapping and ruin of women. IV. The international slave trade in girls. V. Atrocities, brutalities, and unnatural crimes.

That is what I call sexual criminality, as opposed to sexual immorality. It flourishes in all its branches on every side to an extent of which even those specially engaged in rescue work have but little idea. Those who are constantly engaged in its practice naturally deny its existence. But I speak of that which I do know, not from hearsay or rumour, but of my own personal knowledge.

HOW THE FACTS WERE VERIFIED

When the Criminal Law Amendment Bill was talked out just before the defeat of the Ministry it became necessary to rouse public attention to the necessity for legislation on this painful subject. I undertook an investigation into the facts. The evidence taken before the House of Lords' Committee in 1882 was useful, but the facts were not up to date: members said things had changed since then, and the need for legislation had passed. It was necessary to bring the information up to date, and that duty—albeit with some reluctance—I resolutely undertook. For four weeks, aided by two or three coadjutors of whose devotion and self-sacrifice, combined with a rare instinct for investigation and a singular personal fearlessness, I cannot speak too highly, I have been exploring the London Inferno. It has been a strange and unexampled experience. For a month I have oscillated between the noblest and the meanest of mankind, the saviours and the destroyers of their race, spending hours alternately in brothels and hospitals, in the streets and in refuges, in the company of procuresses and of bishops.

London beneath the gas glare of its innumerable lamps became, not like Paris in 1793—"a naphtha-lighted city of Dis" — but a resurrected and magnified City of the Plain, with all the vices of Gomorrah, daring the vengeance of long-suffering Heaven. It seemed a strange, inverted world, that in which I lived those terrible weeks—the world of the streets and of the brothel. It was the same, yet not the same, as the world of business and the world of politics. I heard of much the same people in the house of ill-fame as those of whom you hear in caucuses, in law courts, and on Change. But all were judged by a different standard, and their relative importance was altogether changed. It was as if the position of our world had suddenly been altered, and you saw most of the planets and fixed stars in different combinations, and of altogether different magnitudes, so that at first it was difficult to recognize them. For the house of evil fame has its own ethics, and the best man in the world—the first of Englishmen, in the estimation of the bawd—is often one of whom society knows nothing and cares less. To hear statesmen reckoned up from the standpoint of the brothel is at first almost as novel and perplexing an experience as it is to hear judges and Queen's Counsel praised or blamed, not for their judicial acumen and legal lore, but for their addiction to unnatural crimes or their familiarity with obscene literature. After a time the eye grows familiar with the foul and poisonous air, but at the best you wander in a Circe's isle, where the victims of the foul enchantress's wand meet you at every turn.

But with a difference, for whereas the enchanted in olden time had the heads and the voices and the bristles of swine, while the heart of a man was in them still, these have not put on in outward form "the inglorious likeness of a beast," but are in semblance as other men, while within there is only the heart of a beast—bestial, ferocious, and filthy beyond the imagination of decent men. For days and nights it is as if I had suffered the penalties inflicted upon the lost souls in the Moslem hell, for I seemed to have to drink of the purulent matter that flows from the bodies of the damned. But the sojourn in this hell has not been fruitless. The facts which I and my coadjutors have verified I now place on record at once as a revelation and a warning—a revelation of the system, and a warning to those who may be its victims. In the statement which follows I give no names and I omit addresses. My purpose was not to secure the punishment of criminals but to lay bare the working of a great organization of crime. But as a proof of good faith, and in order to substantiate the accuracy of every statement contained herein, I am prepared after an assurance has been given me that the information so afforded will not be made use of either for purposes of individual exposure or of criminal proceedings, to communicate the names, dates, localities referred to, together with full and detailed explanations of the way in which I secured the information, in confidence to any of the following persons:—

His Grace the Archbishop of Canterbury, The Cardinal Archbishop of Westminster, Mr. Samuel Morley, M.P., The Earl of Shaftesbury, The Earl of Dalhousie, as the author of the Criminal Law Amendment Bill, and Mr. Howard Vincent, ex-Director of the Criminal Investigation Department.

I do not propose to communicate this information to any member of the executive Government, as the responsibilities of their position might render it impossible for them to give the requisite assurance as to the confidential character of my communication. More than this I could not do unless I was prepared (1) to violate the confidence reposed in me in the course of my investigation, and (2) to spend the next six weeks of my life as a witness in the Criminal Court. This I absolutely refuse to do. I am an investigator; I am not an informer.

THE VIOLATION OF VIRGINS

This branch of the subject is one upon which even the coolest and most scientific observer may well find it difficult to speak dispassionately in a spirit of calm and philosophic investigation. The facts, however, as they have been elucidated in the course of a careful and painstaking inquiry are so startling, and the horror which they excite so overwhelming, that it is doubly necessary to approach the subject with a scepticism proof against all but the most overwhelming demonstration. It is, however, a fact that there is in full operation among us a system of which the violation of virgins is one of the ordinary incidents; that these virgins are mostly of tender age, being too young in fact to understand the nature of the crime of which they are the unwilling victims; that these outrages are constantly perpetrated with almost absolute impunity; and that the arrangements for procuring, certifying, violating, repairing, and disposing of these ruined victims of the lust of London are made with a simplicity and efficiency incredible to all who have not made actual demonstration of the facility with which the crime can be accomplished.

To avoid misapprehension, I admit that the vast majority of those who are on the streets in London have not come there by the road of organized rape. Most women fall either by the seduction of individuals or by the temptation which well-dressed vice can offer to the poor. But there is a minority which has been as much the victim of violence as were the Bulgarian maidens with whose wrongs Mr. Gladstone made the world ring some eight years ago. Some are simply snared, trapped and outraged either when under the influence of drugs or after a prolonged struggle in a locked room, in which the weaker succumbs to sheer downright force. Others are regularly procured; bought at so much per head in some cases, or enticed under various promises into the fatal chamber from which they are never allowed to emerge until they have lost what woman ought to value more than life. It is to this department of the subject that I now address myself.

Before beginning this inquiry I had a confidential interview with one of the most experienced officers who for many years was in a position to possess an intimate acquaintance with all phases of London crime. I asked him, "Is it or is it not a fact that, at this moment, if I were to go to the proper houses, well introduced, the keeper would, in return for money down, supply me in due time with a maid—a genuine article, I mean, not a mere prostitute tricked out as a virgin, but a girl who had never been seduced?" "Certainly," he replied without a moment's hesitation. "At what price?" I continued. "That is a difficult question," he said. "I remember one case which came under my official cognizance in Scotland-yard in which the price agreed upon was stated to be £20. Some parties in Lambeth undertook to deliver a maid for that sum to a house of ill fame, and I have no doubt it is frequently done all over London."

"But, "I continued, "are these maids willing or unwilling parties to the transaction—that is, are they really maiden, not merely in being each a virgo intacta in the physical sense, but as being chaste girls who are not consenting parties to their seduction? " He looked surprised at my question, and then replied emphatically: "Of course they are rarely willing, and as a rule they do not know what they are coming for." "But," I said in amazement, "then do you mean to tell me that in very truth actual rapes, in the legal sense of the word, are constantly being perpetrated in London on unwilling virgins, purveyed and procured to rich men at so much a head by keepers of brothels?" "Certainly," said he, "there is not a doubt of it." "Why, "I exclaimed, "the very thought is enough to raise hell." "It is true," he said; "and although it ought to raise hell, it does not even raise the neighbours."

"But do the girls cry out?" "Of course they do. But what avails screaming in a quiet bedroom? Remember, the utmost limit of howling or excessively violent screaming, such as a man or woman would make if actual murder was being attempted, is only two minutes, and the limit of screaming of any kind is only five. Suppose a girl is being outraged in a room next to your house. You hear her screaming, just as you are dozing to sleep. Do you get up, dress, rush downstairs, and insist on admittance? Hardly. But suppose the screams continue and you get uneasy, you begin to think whether you should not do something? Before you have made up your mind and got dressed the screams cease, and you think you were a fool for your pains." "But the policeman on the beat?" "He has no right to interfere, even if he heard anything. Suppose that a constable had a right to force his way into any house where a woman screamed fearfully, policemen would be almost as regular attendants at childbed as doctors. Once a girl gets into such a house she is almost helpless, and may be ravished with comparative safety." "But surely rape is a felony punishable with penal servitude. Can she not prosecute?" "Whom is she to prosecute? She does not know her assailant's name. She might not even be able to recognize him if she met him outside. Even if she did, who would believe her? A woman who has lost her chastity is always a discredited witness. The fact of her being in a house of ill fame would possibly be held to be evidence of her consent. The keeper of the house and all the servants would swear she was a consenting party; they would swear that she had never screamed, and the woman would be condemned as an adventuress who wished to levy black mail." "And this is going on to-day?" "Certainly it is, and it will go on, and you cannot help it, as long as men have money, procuresses are skilful, and women are weak and inexperienced."

VIRGINS WILLING AND UNWILLING.

So startling a declaration by so eminent an authority led me to turn my investigations in this direction. On discussing the matter with a well-known member of Parliament, he laughed and said : "I doubt the unwillingness of these virgins. That you can contract for maids at so much a head is true enough. I myself am quite ready to supply you with 100 maids at £25 each, but they will all know very well what they are about. There are plenty of people among us entirely devoid of moral scruples on the score of chastity, whose daughters are kept straight until they are sixteen or seventeen, not because they love virtue, but solely because their virginity is a realizable asset, with which they are taught they should never part except for value received. These are the girls who can be had at so much a head ; but it is nonsense to say it is rape ; it is merely the delivery as per contract of the asset virginity in return for cash down. Of course there may be some cases in which the girl is really unwilling, but the regular supply comes from those who take a strictly businesslike view of the saleable value of their maidenhead."

My interlocutor referred me to a friend whom he described as the first expert on the subject, an evergreen old gentleman to whom the brothels of Europe were as familiar as Notre Dame and St. Paul's. This specialist, however, entirely denied that there was such a thing as the procuring of virgins, willing or unwilling, either here or on the Continent. Maidenheads, he maintained, were not assets that could be realized in the market, but he admitted that there were some few men whose taste led them to buy little girls from their mothers in order to abuse them. My respect for this "eminent authority " diminished, however, on receiving his assurance that all Parisian and Belgian brothels were managed so admirably that no minors could be harboured, and that no English girls were ever sent to the Continent for immoral purposes. Still even he admitted that little girls were bought and sold for vicious purposes, and this unnatural combination of slave trade, rape, and unnatural crime seemed to justify further inquiry.

I then put myself into direct and confidential communication with brothel-keepers in the West and East of London and in the provinces. Some of these were still carrying on their business, others had abandoned their profession in disgust, and were now living a better life. The information which I received from them was, of course, confidential. I am not a detective, and much of the information which I received was given only after the most solemn pledge that I would not violate their confidence, so as to involve them in a criminal prosecution. It was somewhat unfortunate that this inquiry was only set on foot after the prosecution of Mrs. Jefferies. The fine inflicted on her has struck momentary awe into the heart of the thriving community of "introducers." They could accommodate no one but their old customers. A new face, suggested Mr. Minahan, and an inquiry for virgins or little girls by one who had not given his proofs, excited suspicion and alarm. But, aided by some trustworthy and experienced friends, I succeeded after a time in overcoming the preliminary obstacle so as to obtain sufficient evidence as to the reality of the crime.

THE CONFESSIONS OF A BROTHEL-KEEPER

Here, for instance, is a statement made to me by a brothel keeper, who formerly kept a noted House in the Mile-end road, but who is now endeavouring to start life afresh as an honest man. I saw both him and his wife, herself a notorious prostitute whom he had married off the streets, where she had earned her living since she was fourteen:—

Maids, as you call them—fresh girls as we know them in the trade—are constantly in request, and a keeper who knows his business has his eyes open in all directions, his stock of girls is constantly getting used up, and needs replenishing, and he has to be on the alert for likely "marks" to keep up the reputation of his house. I have been in my time a good deal about the country on these errands. The getting of fresh girls takes time, but it is simple and easy enough when, once you are in it. I have gone and courted girls in the country under all kinds of disguises, occasionally assuming the dress of a parson, and made them believe that I intended to marry them, and so got them in my power to please a good customer. How is it done? Why, after courting my girl for a time, I propose to bring her to London to see the sights. I bring her up, take her here and there, giving her plenty to eat and drink—especially drink. I take her to the theatre, and then I contrive it so that she loses her last train. By this time she is very tired, a little dazed with the drink and excitement, and very frightened at being left in town with no friends. I offer her nice lodgings for the night: she goes to bed in my house, and then the affair is managed. My client gets his maid, I get my £10 or £20 commission, and in the morning the girl, who has lost her character, and dare not go home, in all probability will do as the others do, and become one of my "marks"—that is, she will make her living in the streets, to the advantage of my house. The brothel keeper's profit is, first, the commission down for the price of a maid, and secondly, the continuous profit of the addition of a newly seduced, attractive girl to his establishment. That is a fair sample case of the way in which we recruit. Another very simple mode of supplying maids is by breeding them. Many women who are on the streets have female children. They are worth keeping. When they get to be twelve or thirteen they become merchantable. For a very likely "mark" of this kind you may get as much as £20 or £40. I sent my own daughter out on the streets from my own brothel. I know a couple of very fine little girls now who will be sold before very long. They are bred and trained for the life. They must take the first step some time, and it is bad business not to make as much out of that as possible. Drunken parents often sell their children to brothel keepers. In the East-end, you can always pick up as many fresh girls as you want. In one street in Dalston you might buy a dozen. Sometimes the supply is in excess of the demand, and you have to seduce your maid yourself, or to employ some one else to do it, which is bad business in a double sense. There is a man called S—— whom a famous house used to employ to seduce young girls and make them fit for service when there was no demand for maids and there was a demand for girls who had been seduced. But as a rule the number seduced ready to hand is ample, especially among very young children. Did I ever do anything else in the way of recruiting? Yes. I remember one case very well. The girl, a likely "mark," was a simple country lass living at Horsham. I had heard of her, and I went down to Horsham to see what I could do. Her parents believed that I was in regular business in London, and they were very glad when I proposed to engage their daughter. I brought her to town and made her a servant in our house. We petted her and made a good deal of her, gradually initiated her into the kind of life it was; and then I sold her to a young gentleman for £15. When I say that I sold her, I mean that he gave me the gold and I gave him the girl, to do what he liked with. He took her away and seduced her. I believe he treated her rather well afterwards, but that was not my affair. She was his after he paid for her and took her away. If her parents had inquired, I would have said that she had been a bad girl and run away with a young man. How could I help that? I once sold a girl twelve years old for £20 to a clergyman, who used to come to my house professedly to distribute tracts. The East is the great market for the children who are imported into West-end houses, or taken abroad wholesale when trade is brisk. I know of no West-end houses, having always lived at Dalston or thereabouts, but agents pass to and fro in the course of business. They receive the goods, depart, and no questions are asked. Mrs. S., a famous procuress, has a mansion at —————, which is one of the worst centres of the trade, with four other houses in other districts, one at St. John's-wood. This lady, when she discovers ability, cultivates it—that is, if a comely young girl of fifteen falls into her net, with some intelligence, she is taught to read and write, and to play the piano.

THE LONDON SLAVE MARKET

This brothel-keeper was a smart fellow, and had been a commercial traveller once, but drink had brought him down. Anxious to test the truth of his statement, I asked him, through a trusty agent, if he would undertake to supply me in three days with a couple of fresh girls, maids, whose virginity would be attested by a doctor's certificate. At first he said that it would require a longer time. But on being pressed, and assured that money was no object, he said that he would make inquiries, and see what could be done. In two days I received from the same confidential source an intimation that for £10 commission he would undertake to deliver to my chambers, or to any other spot which I might choose to select, two young girls, each with a doctor's certificate of the fact that she was a virgo intacta. Hesitating to close with this offer, my agent received the following telegram:— "I think all right. I am with parties. Will tell you all to-morrow about twelve o'clock." On calling H— said:—
I will undertake to deliver at your rooms within two days two children at your chambers. Both are the daughters of brothel keepers whom I have

known and dealt with, and the parents are willing to sell in both cases. I represented that they were intended for a rich old gentleman who had led a life of debauchery for years. I was suspected of baby-farming—that is, peaching, at first, and it required all my knowledge of the tricks of the trade to effect my purpose. However, after champagne and liquors, my old friend G——, M——lane, Hackney, agreed to hand over her own child, a pretty girl of eleven, for £5. if she could get no more. The child was virgo intacta, so far as her mother knew. I then went to Mrs. N——, of B——street, Dalston, (B—— street is a street of brothels from end to end). Mrs. N—— required little persuasion, but her price was higher. She would not part with her daughter under £5 or £10, as she was pretty and attractive, and a virgin, aged thirteen, who would probably fetch more in the open market. These two children I could deliver up within two days if the money was right. I would, on the same conditions, undertake to deliver half a dozen girls, ages varying from ten to thirteen, within a week or ten days.

I did not deem it wise to carry the negotiations any further. The purchase price was to be paid on delivery, but it was to be returned if the girls were found to have been tampered with.

That was fairly confirmatory evidence of the existence of the traffic to which official authority has pointed; but I was not content. Making inquiries at the other end of the town, by good fortune I was brought into intimate and confidential communication with an ex-brothel keeper. When a mere girl she had been seduced by Colonel S——, when a maidservant at Petersfield, and had been thrown upon the streets by that officer at Manchester. She had subsequently kept a house of ill fame at a seaport town, and from thence had gravitated to the congenial neighbourhood of Regent's Park. There she had kept a brothel for several years. About a year ago, however, she was picked up, when in a drunken fit, by some earnest workers, and after a hard struggle was brought back to a decent and moral life.

She was a woman who bore traces of the rigorous mill through which she had passed. Her health was impaired; she looked ten years older than her actual age, and it was with the greatest reluctance she could be prevailed upon to speak of the incidents of her previous life, the horror of which seemed to cling to her like a nightmare. By dint of patient questioning, however, and the assurance that I would not criminate either herself or any of her old companions, she became more communicative, and answered my inquiries. Her narrative was straightforward; and I am fully convinced it was entirely genuine. I have since made strict inquiries among those who see her daily and know her most intimately, and I am satisfied that the woman was speaking the truth. She had no motive to deceive, and she felt very deeply the shame of her awful confession, which was only wrung from her by the conviction that it might help to secure the prevention of similar crimes in the future.

HOW GIRLS ARE BOUGHT AND RUINED

Her story, or rather so much of it as is germane to the present inquiry, was somewhat as follows:—

As a regular thing, the landlady of a bad house lets her rooms to gay women and lives on their rent and the profits on the drink which they compel their customers to buy for the good of the house. She may go out herself or she may not. If business is very heavy, she will have to do her own share, but us a rule she contents herself with keeping her girls up to the mark, and seeing that they at least earn enough to pay their rent, and bring home sufficient customers to consume liquor enough to make it pay. Girls often shrink from going out, and need almost to be driven into the streets. If it was not for gin and the landlady they could never carry it on. Some girls I used to have would come and sit and cry in my kitchen and declare that they could not go out, they could not stand the life. I had to give them a dram and take them out myself, and set them agoing again, for if they did not seek gentlemen where was I to get my rent? Did they begin willingly? Some; others had no choice. How had they no choice? Because they never knew anything about it till the gentleman was in their bedroom, and then it was too late. I or my girls would entice fresh girls in, and persuade them to stay out too late till they were locked out, and then a pinch of snuff in their beer would keep them snug until the gentleman had his way. Has that happened often? Lots of times. It is one of the ways by which you keep your house up. Every woman who has an eye to business is constantly on the lookout for likely girls. Pretty girls who are poor, and who have either no parents or are away from home, are easiest picked up, How is it done? You or your decoy find a likely girl, and then you track her down. I remember I once went a hundred, miles and more to pick up a girl. I took a lodging close to the board school, where I could see the girls go backwards and forwards every day. I soon saw one that suited my fancy. She was a girl of about thirteen, tall and forward for her age, pretty, and likely to bring business. I found out she lived with her mother. I engaged her to be my little maid at the lodgings where I was staying. The very next day I took her off with me to London and her mother never saw her again. What became of her? A gentleman paid me £13 for the first of her, soon after she came to town. She was asleep when he did it—sound asleep. To tell the truth, she was drugged. It is often done. I gave her a drowse. It is a mixture of laudanum and something else. Sometimes chloroform is used, but I always used either snuff or laudanum. We call it drowse or black draught, and they lie almost as if dead, and the girl never knows what has happened till morning. And then? Oh! then she cries a great deal from pain, but she is 'mazed, and hardly knows what has happened except that she can hardly move from pain. Of course we tell her it is all right; all girls have to go through it some time, that she is through it now without knowing it, and that it is no use crying. It will never be undone for all the crying in the world. She must now do as the others do. She can live like a lady, do as she pleases, have the best of all that is going, and enjoy herself all day. If she objects, I scold her and tell her she has lost her character, no one will take her in; I will have to turn her out on the streets as a bad and ungrateful girl. The result is that in nine cases out of ten, or ninety-nine out of a hundred, the child, who is usually usually under fifteen, frightened and friendless, her head aching with the effect of the drowse and full of pain and horror, gives up all hope, and in a week she is one of the attractions of the house. Yon say that some men say this is never done. Don't believe them; if these people spoke the truth, it might be found that they had done it themselves. Landladies who wish to thrive must humour their customers. If they want a maid we must get them one, or they will go elsewhere. We cannot afford to lose their custom; besides, after the maid is seduced, she fills up vacancies caused by disease or drink. There are very few brothels which are not occasionally recruited in that way. That case which I mentioned was by no means exceptional; in about seven years I remember selling two maids for £20 each, one at £16, one at £15, one at £13 and others for less. Of course, where I bought I paid less than that. The difference represented my profit, commission, and payment for risk in procuring, drugging, andc.

BUYING GIRLS AT THE EAST-END

This experienced ex-procuress assured me that if she were to return to her old trade she would have no difficulty in laying her hands, through the agency of friends and relatives still in the trade, upon as many young girls as she needed. No house begins altogether with maids, but steps are at once taken to supply one or two young girls to train in. She did not think the alarm of the Jefferies trial had penetrated into the strata where she used to work. But said I, "Will these children be really maids, or will it merely be a plant to get off damaged articles under that guise? " Her reply was significant. "You do not know how it is done. Do you think I would buy a maid on her word? You can soon find out, if you are in the business, whether a child is really fresh or not. You have to trust the person who sells, no doubt, to some extent, but if you are in the trade they would not deceive you in a matter in which fraud can be so easily detected. If one house supplied another with girls who had been seduced, at the price of maids, it would get out, and their reputation would suffer. Besides you do not trust them very far. Half the commission is paid down on delivery, the other half is held over until the truth is proved."

"How is that done?"

"By a doctor or an experienced midwife. If you are dealing with a house you trust, you take their doctor's certificate. If they trust you they will accept the verdict of your doctor." "Does the girl know why you are taking her away?" "Very seldom. She thinks she is going to a situation. When she finds out, it is too late. If she knew what it meant she either would not come or her readiness would give rise to a suspicion that she was not the article you wanted— that, in fact, she was no better than she should be." "Who are these girls?" "Orphans, daughters of drunken parents, children of prostitutes, girls whose friends are far away." "And their price?" "In the trade from £3 to £5 is, I should think, a fair thing. But if you doubt it I will make inquiries, if you like, in my old haunts and tell you what can be done next week."

As there is nothing like inquiry on the spot, I commissioned her to inquire as to the maids then in stock or procurable at short notice by a single bad house in the East of London, whose keeper she knew. The reply was businesslike and direct. If she wanted a couple of maids for a house in the country three would be brought to Waterloo railway station next Saturday at three, from whom two could be selected at £5 per head. One girl, not very pretty, about thirteen, could be had at only at £3. Offer to be accepted or confirmed by letter—which of course never arrived.

A GIRL ESCAPES AFTER BEING SOLD

Being anxious to satisfy myself as to the reality of these transactions, I instructed a thoroughly trustworthy woman to proceed with this ex-keeper to the house in question, and see if she could see any of the children whose price was quoted like that of lambs at so much a head. The woman of the house was somewhat suspicious, owing to the presence of a stranger, but after some conversation she said that she had one fresh girl within reach, whom she would make over at once if they could come to terms. The girl was sent for, and duly appeared. She was told that she was to have a good situation in the country within a few miles of London. She said that she had been brought up at a home at Streatham, had been in service, but had been out of a place for three weeks. She was a pleasant, bright-looking girl, who seemed somewhat nervous when she heard so many inquiries and the talk about taking her into the country. The bargain, however, was struck. The keeper had to receive £2 down, and another sovereign when the girl was proved a maid. The money was paid, the girl handed over, but something said had alarmed her, and she solved the difficulty of disposing of her by making her escape. My friend who witnessed the whole transaction, and whose presence probably contributed something to the difficulty of the bargain, assures me that there was no doubt as to the sale and transfer of the girl. "Her escape," said the ex-keeper, "is one of the risks of the trade. If I had been really in for square business, I should never have agreed to take the girl from the house, partly in order to avoid such escape and partly for safety. It is almost invariably the rule that the seller must deliver the girl at some railway station. She is brought to you, placed in your cab or your railway carriage, and it is then your business, and an easy one, to see that she does not escape you. But the risks of delivery at a safe place are always taken by the seller."

A DREADFUL PROFESSION

When I was prosecuting these inquiries at the East-end, I was startled by a discovery made by a confidential agent at the other end of the town. This was nothing less than the unearthing of a house, kept apparently by a highly respectable midwife, where children were taken by procurers to be certified as virgins before violation, and where, after violation, they were taken to be "patched up," and where, if necessary, abortion could be procured. The existence of the house was no secret. It was well known in the trade, and my agent was directed thither without much ado by a gay woman with whom he had made a casual acquaintance. No doubt the respectable old lady has other business of a less doubtful character, but in the trade her repute is unrivalled, first as a certificator of virginity, and secondly for the adroitness and skill with which she can repair the laceration caused by the subsequent outrage.

That surely was sufficiently horrible. Yet there stood the house, imperturbably respectable in its outward appearance, apparently an indispensable adjunct of modern civilization, its experienced proprietress maintaining confidential relations with the "best houses" in the West-end. This repairer of damaged virgins is not a procuress. Her mission is remedial. Her premises are not used for purposes of violation. She knows where it is done, but she cannot prevent that. What she does is to minimize pain and repair as effectively as possible the ravages of the lust which she did not create, and which she cannot control. But she is a wise woman, whom great experience has taught many secrets, and if she would but speak! Not that she is above giving a hint to those who seek her advice as to where little children can best be procured. A short time ago, she says, there was no difficulty. "Any of these houses," mentioning several of the best known foreign and English houses in the West and North-west, "would, supply children, but at present they are timid. You need to be an old customer to be served. But, after all, it is expensive getting young girls for them. If you really have a fancy that way, why do you not do as Mr. ———— does ? It is cheaper, simpler, and safer." "And how does Mr. ———— do, and who is Mr. ———— ?" "Oh, Mr. ———— is a gentleman who has a great penchant for little girls. I do not know how many I have had to repair after him. He goes down to the East-end and the City, and watches when the girls come out of shops and factories for lunch or at the end of the day. He sees his fancy and marks her down. It takes a little time, but he wins the child's confidence. One day he proposes a little excursion to the West. She consents. Next day I have another subject, and Mr. ———— is off with another girl." "And what becomes of the subjects on which you display your skill?" "Some go home, others go back to their situations, others again are passed on to those who have a taste for second-hand articles," and the good lady intimated that if my agent had such a taste, she was not without hopes that she might be able to do a little trade.

WHY THE CRIES OF THE VICTIMS ARE NOT HEARD

At this point in the inquiry, the difficulty again occurred to me how was it possible for these outrages to take place without detection. The midwife, when questioned, said there was no danger. Some of the houses had an underground room, from which no sound could be heard, and that, as a matter of fact, no one ever had been detected. The truth about the underground chambers is difficult to ascertain. Padded rooms for the purpose of stifling the cries of tortured victims of lust and brutality are familiar enough on the Continent. "In my house," said a most respectable lady, who keeps a villa in the west of London, "you can enjoy the screams of the girl with the certainty that no one else hears them but yourself." But to enjoy to the full the exclusive luxury of revelling in the cries of the immature child, it is not necessary to have a padded room, a double chamber, or an underground room. "Here," said the keeper of a fashionable villa, where in days bygone a prince of the blood is said to have kept for some months one of his innumerable sultanas, as she showed her visitor over the well-appointed rooms, "Here is a room where you can be perfectly secure. The house stands in its own grounds. The walls are thick, there is a double carpet on the floor. The only window which fronts upon the back garden is doubly secured, first with shutters and then with heavy curtains. You lock the door and then you can do as you please. The girl may scream blue murder, but not a sound will be heard. The servants will be far away in the other end of the house. I only will be about seeing that all is snug." "But," remarked her visitor, "if you hear the cries of the child, you may yourself interfere, especially if, as may easily happen, I badly hurt and in fact all but kill the girl" "You will not kill her," she answered, "you have too much sense to kill the girl. Anything short of that, you can do as you please. As for me interfering, do you think I do not know my business?"

Flogging, both of men and women, goes on regularly in ordinary rooms, but the cry of the bleeding subject never attracts attention from the outside world. What chance is there, then, of the feeble, timid cry of the betrayed child penetrating the shuttered and curtained windows, or of moving the heart of the wily watcher—the woman whose business it is to secure absolute safety for her client. When means of stifling a cry—a pillow, a sheet, or even a pocket handkerchief—lie all around, there is practically no danger. To some men, however, the shriek of torture is the essence of their delight, and they would not silence by a single note the cry of agony over which they gloat.

NO ROOM FOR REPENTANCE.

Whether the maids thus violated in the secret chambers of accommodation houses are willing or unwilling is a question on which a keeper shed a flood of light by a very pertinent and obvious remark : "I have never had a maid seduced in my house," he said, "unless she was willing. They are willing enough to come to my house to be seduced, but when the man comes they are never willing." And she proceeded to illustrate what she meant by descriptions of scenes which had taken place in her house when girls, who according to her story had implored her to allow them to be seduced in her rooms, had when the supreme moment arrived repented their willingness, and fought tooth and nail, when too late, for the protection of their chastity. To use her familiar phrase, they made "the devil's own row," and on at least one occasion it was evident that the girl's resistance had only been overcome after a prolonged and desperate fight, in which, what with screaming and violence, she was too exhausted to continue the struggle.

That was in the case of a full-grown woman. Children of twelve and thirteen cannot offer any serious resistance. They only dimly comprehend what it all means. Their mothers sometimes consent to their seduction for the sake of the price paid by their seducer. The child goes to the introducing house as a sheep to the shambles. Once there, she is compelled to go through with it. No matter how brutal the man may be, she cannot escape. "If she wanted to be seduced, and came here to be seduced," says the keeper, "I shall see that she does not play the fool. The gentleman has paid for her, and he can do with her what he likes." Neither Rhadamanthus nor Lord Bramwell could more sternly exact the rigorous fulfilment of the stipulations of the contract. "Once she is in my house," said a worthy landlady, "she does not go out till the job is done. She comes in willingly, but no matter how willing she may be to go out, she stays here till my gentleman has done with her. She repents too late when she repents after crossing my threshold."

STRAPPING GIRLS DOWN

In the course of my investigations I heard some strange tales concerning the precautions taken to render escape impossible for the girl whose ruin, with or without her consent, has been resolved upon. One fact, which is of quite recent occurrence in a fashionable London suburb, the accuracy of which I was able to verify, is an illustration of the extent to which those engaged in this traffic are willing to go to supply the caprices of their customers. To oblige a wealthy customer who by riot and excess had impaired his vitality to such an extent that nothing could minister to his jaded senses but very young maidens, an eminently respectable lady undertook that whenever the girl was fourteen or fifteen years of age she should be strapped down hand and foot to the four posts of the bedstead, so that all resistance save that of unavailing screaming would be impossible. Before the strapping down was finally agreed upon the lady of the house, a stalwart woman and experienced in the trade, had volunteered her services to hold the virgin down by force while her wealthy patron effected his purpose. That was too much even for him, and the alternative of fastening with straps padded on the under side was then agreed upon. Strapping down for violation used to be a common occurrence in Hall-moon-street and in Anna Rosenberg's brothel at Liverpool. Anything can be done for money, if you only know where to take it.

HOW THE LAW ABETS THE CRIMINAL

The system of procuration, as I have already explained, is reduced to a science. The poorer brothel-keeper hunts up recruits herself, while the richer are supported by their agents. No prudent keeper of an introducing house will receive girls brought by other than her accredited and trusted agents. The devices of these agents are innumerable. They have been known to profess penitence in order to gain access to a home for fallen women, where they thought some Magdalens repenting of their penitence might be secured for their house. They go into workhouses, to see what likely girls are to be had. They use servants' registries. They haunt the doors of gaols when girls in for their first offence are turned adrift on the expiry of their sentences. There are no subterfuges too cunning or too daring for them to resort to in the pursuit of their game. Against their wiles the law offers the child over thirteen next to no protection. If a child of fourteen is cajoled or frightened, or overborne by anything short of direct force or the threat of immediate bodily harm, into however an unwilling acquiescence in an act the nature of which she most imperfectly apprehends, the law steps in to shield her violator. If permission is given, says "Stephen's Digest of the Criminal Law," " the fact that it was obtained by fraud, or that the woman did not understand the nature of the act is immaterial."

A CHILD OF THIRTEEN BOUGHT FOR £5

Let me conclude the chapter of horrors by one incident, and only one of those which are constantly occurring in those dread regions of subterranean vice in which sexual crime flourishes almost unchecked. I can personally vouch for the absolute accuracy of every fact in the narrative.

At the beginning of this Derby week, a woman, an old hand in the work of procuration, entered a brothel in ———— st. M————, kept by an old acquaintance, and opened negotiations for the purchase of a maid. One of the women who lodged in the house had a sister as yet untouched. Her mother was far away, her father was dead. The child was living in the house, and in all probability would be seduced and follow the profession of her elder sister. The child was between thirteen and fourteen, and after some bargaining it was agreed that she should be handed over to the procuress for the sum of £5. The maid was wanted, it was said, to start a house with, and there was no disguise on either side that the sale was to be effected for immoral purposes. While the negotiations were going on, a drunken neighbour came into the house, and so little concealment was then used, that she speedily became aware of the nature of the transaction. So far from being horrified at the proposed sale of the girl, she whispered eagerly to the seller, "Don't you think she would take our Lily? I think she would suit." Lily was her own daughter, a bright, fresh-looking little girl, who was thirteen years old last Christmas. The bargain, however, was made for the other child, and Lily's mother felt she had lost her market.

The next day, Derby Day as it happened, was fixed for the delivery of this human chattel. But as luck would have it, another sister of the child who was to be made over to the procuress heard of the proposed sale. She was living respectably in a situation, and on hearing of the fate reserved for the little one she lost no time in persuading her dissolute sister to break off the bargain. When the woman came for her prey the bird had flown. Then came the chance of Lily's mother. The brothel-keeper sent for her, and offered her a sovereign for her daughter. The woman was poor, dissolute, and indifferent to everything but drink. The father, who was also a drunken man, was told his daughter was going to a situation. He received the news with indifference, without even inquiring where she was going to. The brothel-keeper having thus secured possession of the child, then sold her to the procuress in place of the child whose sister had rescued her from her destined doom for £5—£3 paid down and the remaining £2 after her virginity had been professionally certified. The little girl, all unsuspecting the purpose for which she was destined, was told that she must go with this strange woman to a situation. The procuress, who was well up to her work, took her away, washed her, dressed her up neatly, and sent her to bid her parents good-bye. The mother was so drunk she hardly recognized her daughter. The father was hardly less indifferent. The child left her home, and was taken to the woman's lodging in A——street.

The first step had thus been taken. But it was necessary to procure the certification of her virginity—a somewhat difficult task, as the child was absolutely ignorant of the nature of the transaction which had transferred her from home to the keeping of this strange, but apparently kind-hearted woman. Lily was a little cockney child, one of those who by the thousand annually develop into the servants of the poorer middle-class. She had been at school, could read and write, and although her spelling was extraordinary, she was able to express herself with much force and decision. Her experience of the world was limited to the London quarter in which she had been born. With the exception of two school trips to Richmond and one to Epping Forest, she had never been in the country in her life, nor had she ever even seen the Thames excepting at Richmond. She was an industrious, warm-hearted little thing, a hardy English child, slightly coarse in texture, with dark black eyes, and short, sturdy figure. Her education was slight. She spelled write "right," for instance, and her grammar was very shaky. But she was a loving, affectionate child, whose kindly feeling for the drunken mother who sold her into nameless infamy was very touching to behold. In a little letter of hers which I once saw, plentifully garlanded with kisses, there was the following ill-spelled childish verse:—

As I was in bed Some little forths gave in my head. I forth of one, I forth of two; But first of all I forth of you.

The poor child was full of delight at going to her new situation, and clung affectionately to the keeper who was taking her away—where, she knew not.

The first thing to be done after the child was fairly severed from home was to secure the certificate of virginity without which the rest of the purchase-money would not be forthcoming. In order to avoid trouble she was taken in a cab to the house of a midwife, whose skill in pronouncing upon the physical evidences of virginity is generally recognized in the profession. The examination was very brief and completely satisfactory. But the youth, the complete innocence of the girl, extorted pity even from the hardened heart of the old abortionist. "The poor little thing," she exclaimed. "She is so small, her pain will be extreme. I hope you will not be too cruel with her"— as if to lust when fully roused the very acme of agony on the part of the victim has not a fierce delight. To quiet the old lady the agent of the purchaser asked if she could supply anything to dull the pain. She produced a small phial of chloroform. "This," she said, "is the best. My clients find this much the most effective." The keeper took the bottle, but unaccustomed to anything but drugging by the administration of sleeping potions, she would infallibly have poisoned the child had she not discovered by experiment that the liquid burned the mouth when an attempt was made to swallow it. £1 1s. was paid for the certificate of virginity—which was verbal and not written—while £1 10s. more was charged for the chloroform, the net value of which was probably less than a shilling. An arrangement was made that if the child was badly injured Madame would patch it up to the best of her ability, and then the party left the house.

From the midwife's the innocent girl was taken to a house of ill fame, No. —, P——— street, Regent-street, where, notwithstanding her extreme youth, she was admitted without question. She was taken up stairs, undressed, and put to bed, the woman who bought her putting her to sleep. She was rather restless, but under the influence of chloroform she soon went over. Then the woman withdrew. All was quiet and still. A few moments later the door opened, and the purchaser entered the bedroom. He closed and locked the door. There was a brief silence. And then there rose a wild and piteous cry—not a loud shriek, but a helpless, startled scream like the bleat of a frightened lamb. And the child's voice was heard crying, in accents of terror, "There's a man in the room! Take me home; oh, take me home!"

And then all once more was still.

That was but one case among many, and by no means the worst. It only differs from the rest because I have been able to verify the facts. Many a similar cry will be raised this very night in the brothels of London, unheeded by man, but not unheard by the pitying ear of Heaven—

For the child's sob in the darkness curseth deeper Than the strong man in his wrath.

PART II. THE MAIDEN TRIBUTE OF MODERN BABYLON

(July 7)

I described yesterday a scene which took place last Derby day, in a well known house, within a quarter of a mile of Oxford-circus. It is no means one of the worst instances of the crimes that are constantly perpetrated in London, or even in that very house. The victims of the rapes, for such they are to all intents and purposes, are almost always very young children between thirteen and fifteen. The reason for that is very simple. The law at present almost specially marks out such children as the fair game of dissolute men. The moment a child is thirteen she is a woman in the eye of the law, with absolute right to dispose of her person to any one who by force or fraud can bully or cajole her into parting with her virtue. It is the one thing in the whole world which, if once lost, can never be recovered, it is the most precious thing a woman ever has, but while the law forbids her absolutely to dispose of any other valuables until she is sixteen, it insists upon investing her with unfettered freedom to sell her person at thirteen. The law, indeed, seems specially framed in order to enable dissolute men to outrage these legal women of thirteen with impunity. For to quote again from "Stephen's Digest," a rape in fact is not a rape in law if consent is obtained by fraud from a woman or a girl who was totally ignorant of the nature of the act to which she assented. Now it is a fact which I have repeatedly verified that girls of thirteen, fourteen, and even fifteen, who profess themselves perfectly willing to be seduced, are absolutely and totally ignorant of the nature of the act to which they assent. I do not mean merely its remoter consequences and the extent to which their consent will prejudice the whole of their future life, but even the mere physical nature of the act to which they are legally competent to consent is unknown to them. Perhaps one of the most touching instances of this and the most conclusive was the exclamation of relief that burst from a Birmingham girl of fourteen when the midwife had finished her examination.

"It's all over now," she said, "I am so glad."

"You silly child," said the procuress, "that's nothing. You've not been seduced yet. That is still to come." How could she know any better, never having been taught? All that the procuress had told her was that if she consented to meet a rich gentleman she would get lots of money. Even when an attempt is made to explain that there will be some physical pain, the information is so shrouded in mystery that in cases that have come under my own personal knowledge if the man had run a needle into the girl's thigh and told her that she was seduced, she would have believed it.

THE RESPONSIBILITY OF THE MOTHERS

The ignorance of these girls is almost incredible. It is one of the greatest scandals of Protestant training that parents are allowed to keep their children in total ignorance of the simplest truths of physiology, without even a rudimentary conception of the nature of sexual morality. Catholic children are much better trained; and whatever may be the case in other countries, the chastity of Catholic girls is much greater than that of Protestants in the same social strata. Owing to the soul and body destroying taciturnity of Protestant mothers, girls often arrive at the age of legal womanhood in total ignorance, and are turned loose to contend with all the wiles of the procuress and the temptations of the seducer without the most elementary acquaintance with the laws of their own existence. Experientia docet; but in this case the first experience is too often that of violation. Even after the act has been consummated, all that they know is that they got badly hurt; but they think of it and speak of it exactly in the same way as if it meant no more for them than the pulling out of a tooth. Even more than the scandalous state of the law, the culpable refusal of mothers to explain to their daughters the realities and the dangers of their existence contributes to fill the brothels of London.

RECRUITING FOR THE HOUSE OF EVIL FAME

People imagine that the brothel fills itself. That is a mistake. It is recruited for as diligently as is the army of her Majesty, which is perhaps one of its greatest patrons. "Business is very bad," said Mrs. Jefferies mournfully, a short time before her conviction. "I have been very slack since the Guards went to Egypt." The house of ill-fame is a reservoir of vice fed by a multitude of tributary rills. Possibly one-half of its inmates voluntarily elected to take to the streets as a means of livelihood. But although they are volunteers, they are not left to find their way to their destination by natural selection. Every brothel-keeper worth her salt is a procuress with her eyes constantly on the look-out for likely girls, and she is quite as busy weaving toils in which to ensnare fresh women as she is to command fresh customers. When a keeper has spotted a girl whom, she fancies will be "a good mark" she–for in most cases the creature is of the feminine gender–sets to work to secure her for her service. Decoy girls are laid on to tempt the girl with promises of dress and money. The ordinary formula is that if you come with us you will live like a lady, have plenty of fine clothes, have your own way in everything and do as you please. If the girl listens, she is lost. The toils close round. She calls upon her friends. Some night she stops out after the time her mistress locks the door. She is obliged to return to seek shelter, and before morning she is done for. That is the story of thousands, and it is much the most innocent form of procuration. Almost every house of ill-fame in London is the centre of a network of snares and wiles and "plants," intended to bring in fresh girls. That is part of the regular trade. But there are other methods of procuration much more objectionable. "Gentlemen" who seduce girls under promise of marriage and then desert them are probably not responsible for more than 5 to 10 per cent. of our prostitutes, but so long as it is thought honourable and gentlemanly to ruin a girl's life in order to enjoy half an hour's excitement, it is no use saying anything about that mode of recruiting "the Black Army" of our streets. A small proportion take to it from sheer poverty and absolute despair of evading destitution. Many more adopt it occasionally as a means of supplementing scanty wages.

UNWILLING RECRUITS

But that to which I specially wish to direct attention are the arts by which the keeper secures unwilling victims for her house. The simplest and by far the commonest is to engage a girl for the country by advertisement or otherwise to help in the housework. The child–she is seldom more than fifteen or sixteen–comes up from her country village with her box, and is installed in service. At first nothing is said. Every artifice is used to make the unsuspecting girl believe that she is in a good place with a kind mistress. After a time some smart dress is given her, and she is encouraged to be willing and submissive, by promises of greater liberty and plenty of money. The girl is tempted to drink, and by degrees she is enlightened as to the nature of the house. It is a dreadful awakening. What is she to do? In all London she knows no friend–no one to whom she can appeal. She is never allowed to go outside alone. She dare not speak to the policeman, for he is tipped by her mistress. If she asks to leave she is told she must serve out her term, and then every effort is redoubled to seduce her. If possible she is made drunk, and then when she wakes she discovers her ruin has been accomplished. Her character is gone. Hopeless and desperate, without money, without friends, all avenues of escape closed, she has only one choice. "She must do as the others do"–the great formula–or starve in the streets. No one will believe her story, for when a woman is outraged, by fraud or force, her sworn testimony weighs nothing against the lightest word of the man who perpetrated the crime. She sees on one hand leisure, luxury, on the other blank despair. Thus the brothel acquires a new inmate, and another focus of sin and contagion is added to the streets.

THE STORY OF AN ESCAPE

Within the last month I made the acquaintance of a girl of seventeen, who escaped at the eleventh hour from just such a trap. I interviewed her, as I have interviewed many others, but her story is so striking an illustration of the kind of work that is going on all round us that it is worth while giving it just as she gave it to me, merely premising that I have been able, by independent inquiries at Shoreham and Pimlico, to verify the complete accuracy of her statement:–

My name is A—; I am seventeen years old. Last year, about May, I was living with my grandparents who had brought me up at Shoreham. They were poor people, and as I had grown up they thought that it was well I should go to service. I saw an advertisement of a situation: "Wanted a girl to help in the general work of the house." My grandmother wrote about the situation, and as it seemed satisfactory, it was decided I should go. My mistress had to meet me at Victoria station and take me to my new home. I arrived all safely, and at first I thought everything was going to be all right. Mrs. C— was very kind, and let me go to bed at ten. After a time, however, I began to sea something was wrong. The ladies in the house used to drink very much and keep very late hours. Gentlemen were coming and going till three and four o'clock in the morning. I began to see that I was in a bad house. But when I mentioned it to my mother, who is living a gay life in London, she scolded me, and said she would give me a good hiding if I left my place. Where was I to go to? Besides, I thought I might be servant in a bad house without being bad myself. By degrees Mrs. C. began to hint that I was too good to be a general servant; she would get another girl, and I might be a lady like the others. But the girl who had been there before me used to cry very much and tell me never to do as she had done. "Once I was as good as you, Annie, but now there is my baby, and what can I do?" and then she would cry bitterly. The other two girls, when they were sober, would warn me to beware and not come to such a life as theirs, and wish that they had never taken to the streets. And then they would drink again, and go and paint their faces and prepare to receive visitors. I used to be sent with money to buy drink for them, and many a time I wondered if I might run off and never come back. But I had to bring back either the money or the drink or be taken for a thief. And so I went on day after day. One night Mrs. C. brought me a red silk dress and a new hat, and said she was going to take me out. She got into a cab with me and took me to the Aquarium. There she walked me about and then brought me home again. This she did several times, never letting me get out of her sight, never allowing me to go out of doors except for drink and when she took me to the Aquarium. She became more pressing. She showed me a beautiful pink dress, and promised me that also if I would do as the others did. And when I would not, she called me a fool, and used awful language, and said what pleasure I was missing all from stupidity. Sometimes she would tell the gentlemen to take liberties with me, but I kept them at a distance. One night after I had come in with her from the Aquarium, a gentleman tried to catch hold of me as I was outside the bedroom. I ran as hard as I could downstairs. He came after me, but I got into the kitchen first, and there I barricaded the door with chairs and the table, so that he could not get in. I was nearly distracted and did not know what to do, when I found in my box the back of an old hymn-book my grandfather had used. It had on it the address of General Booth, at the headquarters of the Salvation Army. I thought to myself Mr. Booth must be a good man or he would not have so many halls all over the country, and then I thought perhaps he will help me to get out of this horrible house, as I never knew what might happen any night. So I waited quietly all that night, never taking off my clothes. It was usually four o'clock before the house was quiet. As soon as they all seemed to be asleep, I waited till nearly six, and then I crept to the door, opened it, and stole softly away, not even daring to close the door. I only knew one address in all London–101, Queen Victoria-street; where that was I did not know. I walked out blindly till I met a policeman, and he told me the right direction. I walked on and on; it was a long way; I was very tired. I had had no sleep all night, and I feared at any moment to be overtaken and brought back. My red silk dress was rather conspicuous, and I did not know if, even after I got there, whether Mr. Booth would help me. But I felt sure he was a good man, and I walked on and on. The bad house was in Gloucester-street, Pimlico, and it was nearly half-past seven when I got to Queen Victoria-street. The headquarters were closed. I stood waiting outside, wondering if, after all, I might have to go back. At last some one came, and they took care of me, and sent me to their home, and then took me back to Shoreham, where I am now living.

On inquiry at the Salvation Army I found this story, so far as they were concerned, was strictly correct. They give the girl a good character, and say that her grandparents are very respectable, honest people at Shoreham.

They sent to the brothel after hearing her story, and insisted on receiving her box. At first the woman demurred, but on being threatened with exposure reluctantly gave up the box, wishing "the little hussy had broken her neck in getting out of the window when she ran away in that fashion." The girl is now engaged to be married, and, so far as one could judge, seemed a thoroughly modest, respectable young woman. But for the accident of the hymn-book, there is little doubt that she would months ago have been a regular prostitute.

It is significant of the tenacity with which these procuresses cling to their prey, that at the time of Brighton races, when Mrs. C— and her establishment migrated to the seaside, her old mistress came over to Shoreham to try to hire Annie by bribes and threats to return to town. The frightened girl fled to her grandmother, and the woman had to return empty-handed. I have full particulars of names, addresses, dates in my possession, and there is not the least doubt of the substantial accuracy of her story.

TWO STORIES FROM LIFE

In melancholy contrast to the story of Annie is the story of another Annie, a London girl of singularly interesting countenance and pleasing manner. This child did not escape. I met her in one of the innumerable foreign restaurants which serve as houses of assignation in the neighbourhood of Leicester Square.

She was about fifteen years of age, and at the time when I saw her had only been on the streets for a few weeks. Her story, as she told it me with the utmost simplicity and unreserve, was as follows:–

It was about two months since I was seduced. A friend of mine, Jane B—, met me one evening in the street near our house, and asked me if I would go for a walk with her. I said yes, and she proposed to come and have an ice at the very restaurant in which we are now sitting. "It is such a famous shop for ices," she said, "and perhaps we shall see my uncle." I did not know her uncle, nor did I think anything about it, but I walked down to Leicester-square to the restaurant. She asked me to come upstairs to a sitting-room, where we had some ices and some cake. After a time a gentleman came in, whom she said was her uncle; but I found out afterwards he was no more her uncle than I was. He asked us to have some wine and something to eat, and we sat eating and drinking. I had never tasted wine before, but he pressed it on me, and I took one glass and then another, until I think I had four glasses. My head got very queer, and I hardly knew what I did. Then my friend said, ."Annie, you must come upstairs now." "What for?" I said. "Never mind what for," she said ; "you will get lots of money." My head was queer; I did not care what I did, but I remember thinking that it was after no good this going upstairs. She insisted, however, and I went upstairs. The man she called her uncle followed us. She began to undress me. "What are you doing that for?" I said. "You shan't undress me. I don't want to be undressed here." I struggled, and then everything went dizzy. I remember nothing more till I woke and found that I had been undressed and put in bed. The man was in bed with me. I screamed, and begged him to go away. He paid no heed to me, and began to hurt me dreadfully. "Keep quiet, you silly girl," said ——, who stood by the bed; "you will get lots of money." Oh, I was frightened, and the man hurt me so much! But I could do nothing. When it was all over the man gave her £4. She gave me half and kept the other half for herself, as her pay for getting me seduced. I do not know who the man was, and I have never seen him since.

Of course it is obvious that this story rests solely on the authority of the child herself. But there was no reason to question its accuracy. She told me her story very simply in the presence of a friend. It was perfectly natural, and the girl's remembrance of the way in which she had been ruined was very clear. She seemed a girl of excellent disposition, a Sunday scholar, and of refined manners, and with a sweetness of expression unusual in her class. Her companion, a young girl of thirteen, was a child of much greater character and resolution, who, I am glad to say, is now in good hands in the country. Her story was as follows:—

One night a girl I knew came and spoke to me. "Will you come and see a gentleman?" she said. "Me see a gentleman—what do you mean?" said I. "Oh, I forgot," she says; "will you come and take a walk?" I had no objection, so we went for a walk. After a while, she proposed we should go into a house in P— street and get something to eat. We went in, and after we had been there a little time in came a gentleman. He sat down and talked a bit, and then my friend says, "Take off your things, Lizzie." "No, I won't," I said. "Why should I take off my things?" "Don't be a fool," says she, "and do as I tell you, you will get lots of money;" and she began to undress me. I objected, but she was older than I, and stronger, and the man took her side. "Now," she said after she had undressed me, "get into bed with you." "What for?" says I, "for I had no idea what she meant." "Do as I tell you, you little fool, or I will knock you[r] head off you. This gentleman will give you lots of money, pounds and pounds, if you are good; but he won't give you a penny if you are stupid." And she half forced me, half persuaded me, to get into bed. Then the gentleman got into bed. I did not know what he wanted. I was very frightened, and was crying bitterly. Then he began to hurt me, and I yelled at the top of my voice. Madame who kept the house heard me scream, and she came running up. "Vot is you a doin to that von leetle girl?" she asked. "Nothing," said the man; "she has only run a pin into her foot;" and my friend whispered, "Only keep quiet and you shall have it all. I will give you all the money. But mind you won't get off, no matter how you scream." Madame went away, and the man finished me. He gave me £3. 10s.

Lizzie, who told me the above story, is a mere child, thirteen years old last June. Her mother was dead. Her father was a foreman in a City warehouse. She is a girl of great energy and restlessness, affectionate, and I believe she is now doing well. Both of these girls, after being seduced, went on the streets occasionally. It is the first step which costs, and after having lost their virtue, they argued that they might now and then add to their scanty earnings by the easily acquired gold to be earned in the brothel.

PROCURATION IN THE WEST-END

The price of maids is much higher in the West-end than when the virgins are picked up in the East. But the purveying of maidens is done systematically enough. Prices, I should say, rule as follows:–From the wholesale firm of Mdmes. X. and Z., of which I shall speak shortly, £5, at an East-end brothel £10, at the West-end £20. These quotations are actual figures, and have been given me by those who were perfectly willing to fulfil the contract. In all cases they include the maiden's own fee as well as the commission paid to the purveyor. In no case was the slightest objection made to the stipulation that the virginity of the girl should be certified by a doctor before delivery–a fact which entirely disposes of the cry that no business is done excepting in harlots vamped up as virgins for that occasion only. I had a good opportunity of an inside view of procuration as practised in one of the most select and respectable houses in the West, where I had commissioned the mistress to procure me a maid at £20. She told me, of course–as they all do–that she never did such things, that she never had a maid seduced in her house in her life, and would not for the world, even for her oldest customer, consent to allow her house to be used for that purpose. In fact, she went so far as to say that if a girl was seduced in her house she would feel as if she were bound to provide for her in an afterlife. The value of these preliminary assurances may be gauged from the fact that she subsequently undertook to provide me with a maid, and offered me the choice of any room in her house for the purpose of seducing her. She incidentally described a considerable number of girls who had been seduced in her house, and then let me so far into her confidence as to say that she had three procuresses in connection with her house whose duty it was to pick up girls for her customers. I was offered the choice between a nursery governess, a nursemaid, and another girl. I selected the nursery governess, who, I was told, was in a good situation in a gentleman's family near Victoria station. Unfortunately the day when we had to meet her mistress sent her with the children to Hurlingham, and she could not keep her appointment, much to the disappointment of the procuress, who paid no fewer than three visits to the house. Another appointment was made, but they brought a housemaid instead of the governess. I saw her in company with the procuress, a motherly old lady, whose profession was that of charwoman. I had a long and interesting conversation with her, which need not be detailed here. The salient feature of it was the complacency with which the good lady regarded her occupation as procuress. To begin with, she had the excuse of poverty. She was a widow with a large family, and must do something for the children. Her second justification was the assumption that the girls whom she procured would inevitably be seduced, and, said she naively, "If a girl is to be seduced it is better she should be seduced by a gentleman, and get something for it than let herself be seduced by a boy or a young fellow who gives her nothing for it" These two excuses not only satisfied the old lady's conscience, but made her feel that she was quite a benefactor to her sex.

The maid whom she procured for me (although I cannot speak positively as to her virginity, as, owing to the delay of a telegram, my doctor failed to arrive at the trysting-place) was a pretty young girl about fifteen, a very sweet face, and immature figure. She had been crying because Mrs. — had scolded her for dressing like a butterfly instead of wearing black. Her story was that her mother was ill, which I subsequently discovered was true, and she wanted to get £10 to help her in her trouble. She was perfectly willing to be examined by a doctor, for, as the old lady said, "if she is going to be seduced she need not mind seeing a doctor," and her readiness to submit to the examination was at least prima facie evidence of the reality of her claim to be regarded as a maid. The scene with the procuress and the girl was very striking. The old lady trotted out the child, made her stand up, smile, and generally put her through her paces, and showed off her points. The motherly fashion in which she put her arms round the girl's neck, and urged her with kisses and encouragement not to be timid, but to please the gentleman, was sickening beyond expression. It was with great difficulty that I got a few moments alone with the girl. "Why do you want to be seduced?" I asked. "Tell me the truth." "For the money," she. replied, quite simply. "Would you rather have £5 and not be seduced, or the £10 and be seduced?" "Oh, £5 by all means," she said, "and not be seduced." And then the old procuress returned. The girl seemed timid, but whether she was really a maid or not I do not know. When the doctor turned up a second time she did not come, and I have reason to fear that she is no longer likely to pass the ordeal of an examination.

In the course of conversation I found that charwomen are regarded as excellent procuresses. They have the entry into private houses and into shops where many girls are employed. Coming day after day, early in the morning, before the mistress or the manager is about, they have ample opportunities, of which they make the most, to entice young girls to destruction. They make it their duty to allay the fears of the girls as to the consequences of seduction. The old lady was quite eloquent and emphatic in assuring me that a girl never need fear having a child as the result of a first seduction. That is the way in which the descensus Averni is smoothed. "No harm will come the first time" helps the girl to consent, and after she has lost her maiden estate the argument is, "You can go a second time." "It is only the first step that costs," and so the girl gets fairly launched on an immoral life. But in justice to this establishment I must say that they stoutly refused to deliver the girl over to me altogether. "I must restore her to her mother's arms," said the old lady, who in this case had fortified herself with a written certificate from the mother declaring her assent to her daughter's seduction.

A FIRM OF PROCURESSES

The recruiting for the brothel is by no means left to occasional irregular agents. It is a systematized business. Mesdames X. and Z., procuresses, London, is a firm whose address is not to be found in "The Post Office Directory." It exists, however, and its operations are in full swing at this moment. Its members have made the procuration of virgins their speciality. The ordinary house of ill-fame recruits its inmates occasionally by purchase, by contract, by force, or by fraud, but as a rule the ordinary brothel keeper relies for the staple of her commodities upon those who have already been seduced. To oblige a customer they will procure a maid, in many cases passing off as virgins those who had long before bade farewell to the estate of maidenhood; for the tricks of women are innumerable, and the contrivances by which this can be done are numerous and simple. The number of vamped-up virgins which Mrs. Jefferies is currently reported to have procured for her aristocratic clientele in the neighbourhood of the Quadrant is regarded in the profession as one of the most remarkable achievements of the great Chelsea procuress. These are, however, but the tricks of the trade, which in no way concern the object of the present inquiry.
The difference between the firm of Mesdames X. and Z. and the ordinary keeper of an introducing house is that the procuring of maids (which in the case of the latter is occasional) is the constant occupation of their lives. They do nothing else. They keep no house of ill-fame. One of the members of this remarkable firm lives in all the odour of propriety if not of sanctity with her parents; the other, who has her own lodgings, nominally holds a position of trust and of influence in the establishment of a well-known firm in Oxford-street. These things, however, are but as blinds. Their real work, to which they devote every day in the week, is the purveying of maidens to

an extensive and ever-widening circle of customers. The office of the firm is at —, —place, the lodgings of the junior partner, where letters and telegrams are sent and orders received, and the necessary correspondence conducted. Both partners are young, the senior member of the firm being really younger than her partner. The business was started by Miss X—, a young woman of energy and ability and great natural shrewdness almost immediately after her seduction in 1881. She was at that time in her sixteenth year. A girl who had already fallen introduced her to a "gentleman," and pocketed half the price of her virtue as commission. The ease with which her procuress earned a couple of pounds came like a revelation to Miss X., and almost immediately after her seduction she began to look about to find maids for customers and customers for maids. After two years, business had increased to such an extent that she was obliged to take into partnership Miss Z., an older girl, about twenty, of slenderer figure and fairer complexion. At one time Miss Z. gave all her time to the business, but one of their customers suggested that it would look more respectable, and besides increase her opportunities, if she resumed her old position as head of a sewing-room in the establishment alluded to. She accordingly went back to her old quarters and resumed the responsibility of looking after the morals and manners of some score young apprentice girls who come up from the country to learn the business. I am thus precise in giving details not only because the firm is only one of several which have hitherto escaped the attention of the social observer, but because the very existence of such an organized business for the procuration of virgins has been stoutly denied by those who are believed to know what is going on.

HOW ANNIE WAS PROCURED

I heard accidentally of the operations of this famous firm in conversation with a bright-looking young girl about sixteen who was telling me the way in which she was first brought out. "Oh, Miss X. brought me out," she said, "nearly two years ago. I was at that time, as I still am, in a situation as nurse girl. I used to go with the perambulator and the baby to St. James's Park every day. When wheeling the perambulator a nicely-dressed lady used to pass me nearly every day. She used to say, 'Good morning,' and pass on. One day she stopped a little to talk about the baby. 'What a fine child,' says she. 'And are you its nurse?' And then she gave the baby a halfpenny and me a penny, and I thought her a very kind lady indeed. After that she always used to stop and talk, and I used to tell my mistress what a pleasant lady Miss X— was, and how much she liked the baby. 'I would like to see Miss X—' said my mistress. 'Would you not invite her to tea some time?' which I did. Miss X— was, oh! so polite, said, 'Yes, ma'am,' and 'No, ma'am,' and quite pleased my mistress. After that, one day when I was in the park, she came up and said, 'Nance, have you ever had a man?' I did not know exactly what she meant, and said so. She then asked, 'Would you not like to get such a lot of money?' Of course I said, 'Yes.' Then she said, 'I know several girls who have got pounds and pounds, and I can help you to do the same.' 'Can you?' said I, 'that would be very kind.' 'Yes,' she said, 'it is very easy; you only need to have a little game with a gentleman.' 'Oh,' I said, 'I don't want to see a gentleman. What would he do with me?' 'Oh, nothing,' she said. 'But never mind; if you don't like the chance we'll say no more about it.' And then she went away, and I did not see her for some time. I thought a great deal about what she said. I wanted some new clothes. I had not much wages, and she said pounds and pounds could be got quite easily. I did not know what she meant about having fun with a gentleman. One day I saw her again, and she came up to me and said: 'Nance, I am going to give you another chance. Will you go and see a gentleman friend of mine, and you will get pounds, and you can buy new dresses, new hats, and nets, and all kinds of things?' 'But what for?' I asked. 'Never mind what for, you silly girl: he will only have a game with you, and you will be none the worse for it. But look you,' she said, speaking quite sharp, 'I don't want to fool away my time over you. There's that other girl will jump at the chance I've offered you. Say you won't and I'll take her.' And then I said, 'Oh yes, I'll go, I'll go,' and she took me. It was somewhere in the country. We went by train. Miss X— took me. The first time I was very frightened, and when the gentleman began to undress me I cried, for I did not know what he was going to do. So he did nothing that day, but said I must come another time. He was a very kind gentleman, who lived in a fine house and played on the piano. He gave me £5 that time. Miss X— brought me another day, and that time he seduced me, and gave me another £5. I did not cry when he undressed me the second time, but afterwards I screamed. 'Let me go, let me go,' I shouted, all in a tremble, 'and I'll go and work for my living,' and I struggled to get free. 'Child,' said he, angrily, 'don't dirty my shirtsleeves. Don't dirty my shirtsleeves There is a danger of course that the last phrase may be held apply to Candahar, but we prefer to believe that it refers sole to Quetta, whatever you do,' for I was tearing at them to get free. It was of no use, and I was done for." "Who is this Miss X— ? "I asked.

"Miss X–," said Nance, "is the one who gets nearly all the young girls away from here. She is a very clever woman, and persuades girls to meet men." "Do they always know what they are going for?" I asked. "Oh, no," she said; "some do, of course, but others don't." "And these others–when they find out do they get away?" "How can they?" she replied; "Miss X. would knock their heads off if they tried. 'I am not going to have you make a fool of me and of my gentleman,' she says. The girl cannot get away, then–it is too late–and if they make much trouble she says, 'You will be seduced all the same whatever you do, but if you make much row you shan't have a penny.' "And so the girl gives in."

"YOU WANT A MAID DO YOU?"

All this was said with such perfect good faith and simplicity, and without the faintest tinge of animosity towards the procuress, that I was curious to make the acquaintance of so accomplished and vigorous a lady. An interview was arranged without much difficulty for the transaction of business. Unfortunately the senior partner was engaged, but Miss Z—— was at liberty. I explained my business. "Oh, you want a maid, do you?" she said. "I will bring one to-morrow night. The price will be about £5, including commission." "But," said I, "she will have to be certified by a doctor or a midwife as really a maid, otherwise I will not look at her." "All right," she said, "that is not very usual; and you will have to pay the doctor. But I have had to do it before now, and there will be no difficulty about that."

THE ORDER EXECUTED

Next night, promptly at the appointed time, Miss Z—— arrived with her maid. The child was about fourteen, dark, with long black hair and dark eyes. She was not fully grown, and promised if well cared for to develop into a woman of somewhat striking appearance. She was a Birmingham girl, and the London sewing-rooms had not yet robbed her cheeks of the rural bloom. Her story was soon told. She had been sent to ——, in Oxford-street, to learn dressmaking, as an apprentice from the country. She was to serve three months in return for board and lodgings. She received no wages, and was illiterate—reading with difficulty, and not writing at all. She had only been in London three weeks, and she had no pocket money, nor was she able to buy the clothes or boots which she wanted. Miss Z—— had noticed her on her arrival as a likely girl, and suggested that she might make a few pounds by meeting a rich gentleman. Every one did it, she said, and she would get the money she needed without any trouble. The girl, with only the vaguest idea of what was involved in meeting a gentleman, naturally consented, and she was brought to me as willing to be seduced. It was on the Monday that I saw her. On the previous Saturday her mother had died. She was to be buried on the following Tuesday. The idea of the mother lying dead at home while the daughter was being brought out for seduction struck me as so peculiarly ghastly that I could not resist mentioning it to the procuress. "Yes, poor thing," she said, " it is a pity. But stopping in would not bring her mother to life again, so I told her she had better come out." I sent the girl to a midwife. It was this case in which the remarks made by the child after the midwife concluded the examination, to which I have already referred, proved her innocence. The child actually imagined that the seduction had been accomplished when the midwife made her smart. Yet that girl was between fourteen and fifteen years of age, and in the eye of the law had been for nearly two years fully competent to give legal assent to her own ruin.

AN INTERVIEW WITH THE FIRM

I had a long conversation with Mesdames X. and Z. on a subsequent day, as to their business—the way in which it was carried on, and the facility with which they were able to procure subjects. The members of the firm were very sociable and communicative, and in the course of the evening they gave me a good idea of the whole art and mystery of procuration, as practised by its most skilful professors. The following is a report of an interview almost unique in its way:–

"I was told the other day," said I, by way of opening the conversation, "that the demand for maidenheads has rather fallen away of late, owing to the frauds of the procurers. The market has been glutted with vamped-up virgins, of which the supply is always in excess of the demand, and there are fewer inquiries for the genuine article."

"That is not our experience," said the senior partner, a remarkable woman, attractive by the force of her character in spite of the ghastliness of her calling, compared to which that of the common hangman is more honourable. "We do not know anything about vamped virgins. Nor, with so many genuine maids to be had for the taking, do I think it worth while to manufacture virgins. I should say the market was looking up and the demand increasing. Prices may perhaps have fallen, but that is because our customers give larger orders. For instance, Dr. —, one of my friends, who used to take a maid a week at .£10, now takes three a fortnight at from £5, to £7 each."

"What!" I exclaimed; "do you actually supply one gentleman with seventy fresh maids every year?"

"Certainly," said she; "and he would take a hundred if we could get them. But he is so very particular. He will not take a shop-girl, and he always must have a maid over sixteen."

THE PROCURESS LEARNED IN THE LAW

"Why over sixteen?" said I. "Because of the law," she replied; "no one is allowed to take away from her home, or from her proper guardians, a girl who is under sixteen. She can assent to be seduced after she is thirteen, but even if she assented to go, both the keeper of the house where we took her, and my partner and I, would be liable to punishment if she was not over sixteen. Hence my old gentleman, who is very careful, will not look at a girl under sixteen. That diminishes the area from which maids can be drawn. The easiest age to pick them up is fourteen or fifteen. At thirteen they are just out of school, and still more or less babies under the influence of their mothers. But at fourteen and fifteen they begin to get more liberty without getting much more sense; they begin to want clothes and things which money can buy, and they do not understand the value of what they are parting with in order to get it. After a girl gets past sixteen she gets wiser, and is more difficult to secure."

"You seem to know the law," said I, "better than I know it myself."

"Have to," said she promptly. "It's my business. It would never do for me not to know what was safe and what was not. We might get both ourselves and our friends into no end of trouble, if we did not know the law."

"But how do you get to know all these points?" I inquired.

From the newspapers," she replied. "Always read the newspapers, they are useful. Every week I take in two, Lloyd's and the Weekly Dispatch, and I spend the great part of Sunday in reading all the cases in the courts which relate to this subject. There is a case now going on at Walworth, where a man is charged with abducting a girl, fifteen, and it was laid down in court that if she could be proved to be one day over sixteen he was safe. I am watching that case with great interest. All these cases when reported I cut out and put in a book for reference, so that I know pretty well where I am going."

THE SPECIALITY OF THEIR BUSINESS

"Then do you do anything in the foreign trade?" I asked. "Oh, no," she said. "Our business is in maidenheads, not in maids. My friends take the girls to be seduced and take them back to their situations after they have been seduced, and that is an end of it so far as we are concerned. We do only with first seductions, a girl passes only once through our hands, and she is done with. Our gentlemen want maids, not damaged articles, and as a rule they only see them once."

"What comes of the damaged articles?" "They all go back to their situations or their places. But," said the procuress reflectively, "they all go to the streets after a time. When once a girl has been bad she goes again and again, and finally she ends like the rest. There are scarcely any exceptions. Do you remember any, Z.?" The junior partner remembered one or two, but agreed that it was very rare girls ever went straight after once they had been seduced.

"Do they ever have children?"

"Not very often the first time. Of course we tell them that it never happens. Girls are so silly, they will believe anything. That silly little child we brought you, for instance, thought she had been seduced when the midwife touched her. But of course sometimes they get in the family way the first time."

And then," said I, "I suppose they affiliate the child?" "On whom, pray?" said the senior partner, laughing. "We make it a special feature of our business that the maid never knows who is her seducer, and in most cases they never know our address. How can she get to know? I have to take a cook, for instance, next Sunday at church time to Mr.—, who has a place in Bedford-square, and three other places at least all about where maids are delivered. I take the girl in a cab. We drive through, street after street. Then we stop opposite a door and go in. The cook will see a gentleman who maybe with her a few minutes, or he may be with her half an hour. During that time she is naturally somewhat excited and suffers more or less pain. As soon as she is dressed I take her away in a cab and she never sees that gentleman again. Even if she noticed the house, which is doubtful, she does not know the name of its owner, and in many cases the house is merely a brothel. What can she do?" THE FORCING OF UNWILLING MAIDS

"Do the maids ever repent and object to be seduced when the time comes?" "Oh, yes," said Miss X., "sometimes we have no end of trouble with the little fools. You see they often have no idea in the world as to what being seduced is. We do not take much trouble to explain, and it is enough for us if the girl willingly consents to see or to meet or to have a game with a rich gentleman. What meaning she attaches to seeing a gentleman it is not our business to inquire. All that we have to do is to bring her there and see that she does not make a fool of the gentleman when she gets there."

"You always manage it though?" I inquired.

"Certainly," she said. "If a girls makes too much trouble, she loses her maidenhead for nothing instead of losing it for money. The right way to deal with these silly girls is to convince them that now they have come they have got to be seduced, willing or unwilling, and that if they are unwilling, they will be first seduced and then turned into the streets without a penny. Even then they sometimes kick and scream and make no end of a row. You remember Janie," she said, appealing to Miss Z. "Don't I just," said that amiable lady. "You mean that girl we had to hold down?" "Yes," said Miss X. "We had fearful trouble with that girl. She wrapped herself up in the bed-curtains and screamed and fought and made such a rumpus, that I and my friend had to hold her down by main force in bed while she was being seduced."

"Nonsense," I said, "you did not really?"

Didn't we, though?" she replied. "I had to hold one shoulder and she held the other, and even then it was as much as we could do to keep her still. She was mortally terrified, and didn't she scream and yell!" "It gave me such a sickening," said the junior partner, " that I was almost going to chuck up the business, but I got into it again."

THE PROFITS OF A PROCURESS

"It pays, I suppose?" "Oh yes, there is no need for me to go to work. It is only for appearance sake and opportunities. I can leave when I like," said Miss Z., "after I get them started in the morning. We are paid by commission."

"Fifty per cent.? "I asked.

"That depends," said the senior partner. "Taking the average price of a maid at £5, we sometimes take £1; but sometimes we take it all, and merely make the girl a present. It depends upon the trouble which we have, and the character of the girl. Some girls are such sillies."

"How do you mean?"

We'll take Nance, for instance. She was a lightheaded girl who had never fancied money. We got £10 for Nance. If she had got half that, or quarter, it would have turned her head. She would have gone and bought no end of clothes, and her mistress and her mother would have found it out, and Nance would have got into no end of a row. So for Nance's own sake we only gave her a pound, and as we made her stand treat out of that, she had very little left out of her money to play the fool with. But we have been good to Nance, afterwards. I gave her a bonnet, a dress, and a pair of shoes. I should think we have spent £2 over her."

So that she had altogether £3, and you had £7?"

Just so," said Miss X——, "and girls are often like that; we have to save them from themselves by keeping most of the money out of their reach;" and the good lady evidently contemplated herself with the admiration due to a virtue so careful of the interests of the young sillies who place themselves in her experienced hands.

"Tell me," said I, reverting to a previous subject, "when these maids scream so fearfully does no one ever interfere?"

"No; we take them to a quiet place, and the people of the house know us and would not interfere, no matter what noise went on. Often we take them to private houses, and there of course all is safe. The time for screaming is not long. As soon as it is over the girl sees it is no use howling. She gets her money and goes away. We do not need any specially prepared room. Any quiet room in a house where you are known will do. I have never known one case of interference in the four years I have been in the business."

WHERE MAIDS ARE PICKED UP

"Who supplies most of your maids?" "Nurse-girls and shop-girls, although occasionally we get a governess, and sometimes cooks and other servants. We get to know the servants-through-the nurses. Young girls from the country, fresh and rosy, are soon picked up in the shops or as they run errands. But nurse-girls are the great field. My old friend is always saying to me, 'Why don't you pick up nurse-girls, there are any number in Hyde Park every morning, and all virgins.' That is when we have disappointed him, which is not very often."

"But how do you manage to pick up so many?"

The senior partner replied with conscious pride, "It takes time, patience, and experience. Many girls need months before they can be brought in. You need to proceed very cautiously at first. Every morning at this time of the year my friend and I are up at seven, and after breakfast we put a shawl round our shoulders and off we go to scour the park. Hyde Park and the Green Park are the best in the morning; Regent's Park in the afternoon. As we go coasting along, we keep a sharp look out for any likely girl, and having spotted one we make up to her; and week after week we see her as often as possible, until we are sufficiently in her confidence to suggest how easy it is to earn a few pounds by meeting a man. In the afternoon off goes the shawl and on goes the jacket, and we are off on the same quest. Thus we have always a crop of maids ripening, and at any time we can undertake to deliver a maid if we get due notice."

I ORDER FIVE VIRGINS

"Come," said I, in a vein of bravado, "what do you say to delivering me five on Saturday next?"–it was then Wednesday–"I want them to be retailed to my friends. You are the wholesale firm, could you deliver me a parcel of five maids, for me to distribute among my friends, after having them duly certificated?" "Five," she said, "is a large order, I could bring you three that I know of; but five! It is difficult getting so many girls away at the same time from their places. But we will try, although I have never before delivered more than two, or at the most three, at one place. It will look like a boarding-school going to the midwife."

"Never mind that. Let us see what you can do."

And then and there an agreement was made that it should be done. They were to deliver five at £5 a head all round, commission included. But as I was buying wholesale to sell again it was agreed that they would find the girls at a commission of 20s. a head for each certificated virgin, and deliver to me a written pledge, signed with the name and address of each girl, consenting to come at two days' notice to be seduced at any given place for a certain sum down. I had to pay the doctor's fee for examination and make an allowance for cabs, andc.

THE VIRGINS CERTIFIED

The bargain was struck, an arle-penny was paid over, and the procuresses set about preparing for the delivery of their goods the following Saturday. At half-past five o'clock, at a certain point in Marylebone-road, not far from the very fashionable brothel kept by Mrs. B—, I awaited the arrival of the convoy. A few minutes after time I saw Mesdames X. and Z. coming along the streets, but with only three girls. One was tall, pretty, and apparently about sixteen, the other two were younger–somewhat heavy in their build. Two of them were shop girls, being employed in different departments of the well-known firm of – –, the other was learning some milliner's work at another shop. The procuresses were profuse in their apologies. They had been as far as Highgate to make up the quota of the five, but two of the girls could not leave their places on Saturday. They would bring them on Monday without fail. In fact, to atone for their inability to bring five on Saturday, they would bring three on Monday, making six in all. Perhaps also it was better not to make a sensation by having seven women tripping all together into one doctor's. It was safer to have three at a time. They looked hot and tired and had already spent 6s. in cabs. The tall girl had given them a great deal of trouble, but they had got her at last. We went into the doctor's.

None of the three girls knew each other. They were not allowed to speak to each other or even to shake hands. As for knowing my name, the procuresses themselves did not know it. We went into the doctor's. The maids one by one went in to be examined. They made no objection. After their examination was done they signed a formal agreement for their subsequent seduction. To the unutterable disgust of the girls two of them were refused a certificate. The doctor could not say that they were not virgins; but neither of them was technically a virgo intacta. I then gave them 5s. per head for their trouble in coming to be certificated, paid Mesdames X. and Z. their commission on the one certificated virgin and expenses, and departed armed with the following set of documents:–

_____ _____ W.,
June 27, 1885.
This is to certify that I have this day examined — D—, aged 16 years, and have found her a virgin.
— —, M.D.
Agreement.
I hereby agree to let you have me for a present of £3 or £4. I will come to any address if you give me two days' notice.
Name — D —, aged 16.
Address No. 11, — Street, H—
Both the non-certificated signed a similar agreement, differing only in the

name, age, and address. Nothing could be more simple or more businesslike than this transaction, which only differed from the regular operations carried on every day by the firm of firm of Mesdames X. and Z., because for the seduction there was substituted a doctor's examination, and the signature on a slip of paper, giving me the right to call up my virgins at two days' notice.

The doctor, I should state, was in the secret, and consented to undertake the examination solely in order to expose the system of procuration in which less unscrupulous medical men sometimes play a leading part.

The procuresses were much upset at the rejection of two-thirds of their consignment. The girls were very indignant at the reflection upon their chastity–which after all may have been entirely unfounded. But like sensible business people the firm determined to execute their order without more ado. On the following Monday the nursemaids were delivered at the doctor's. Both were virgins. I hold the following certificates and agreements:–

— —, W.,

June 39, 1885.

This is to certify that I have examined — W—, aged 17 years, and — K—, aged 17 years, and have found them both virgins.

— —, M.D.

Agreement.

I hereby agree to let you have me for £ , and will come to any address you send me at two days' notice.

Name, — K—, aged 17.

Address, 24, R— Street.

Agreement.

I hereby agree to let you have me for £ , and will come to any address you send me at two days' notice.

Name, — + (her mark), aged 17.

Address, 318, S — Street.

The sum for which they agreed to sell their chastity was left blank in the original. Thus in six days I had secured three certificated maids and two uncertificated. The tale was still incomplete, and although I was satisfied, the firm insisted upon holding me to my bargain. Five I had ordered and five I should have, but they must have a day or two's grace. Last Friday morning they arrived at the doctor's with no fewer than four girls–three fourteen years old, and one an under-cook of eighteen, from one of the first hotels in the West-end. They had brought four, they explained, lest any of them should fail to pass their examination. Singular to relate, all the younger children were rejected. Only the eighteen-year-old was certificated. "I never saw anything like these young things," said Miss X.; "it is always the young ones who are unable to stand the doctor's examination."

The certificated maid stood out for £5. Here is her certificate and her agreement:–

This is to certify that having examined —— D —— , I have found her to be a virgin. —— —— , M.D., andc.

Agreement.

I hereby agree to let you have me for £5. I will come to any address if you give me two days' notice.

Name, —— D —— , aged 18.

Address,—— Hotel.

I took another agreement from one of the fourteen-year-old uncertificated children for £4, and assured the firm that I was content. They had brought me altogether nine girls in ten days from the receipt of the order, four of whom were certificated as maids and five were rejected. I have now in my possession the agreement for seduction of all the certificated maids and of three of the uncertificated, of the virginity of whom I have very little doubt. In all, I have agreements signed by seven girls varying from fourteen to eighteen years of age, who are ready to be seduced by any one when and where I please, provided only that I give two days' notice, and pay them altogether a sum not less than £24, nor more than £29. Fees, expenses, andc., incurred in procuring these girls cost, say, £10 or £15 more. Altogether I was in a position to retail virgins at £10 each, and make a handsome profit on the transaction.

DELIVERED FOR SEDUCTION

The firm of Mesdames X. and Z. had, however, no intention of allowing me to call up my virgins without their intervention. They had carefully instructed all the girls to give false addresses, in order that I might be compelled to obtain them through the firm. This was a breach of contract on the part of the firm which I had good reason to resent, especially as I only discovered it incidentally by sending a summons to call up some of the girls. The reason for this breach of faith was, they allege, that if I had communicated directly with the girls I might have alarmed their parents or employers, and that it was necessary to do it through them. The real reason was the desire of the firm to make quite sure that they received the fifty per cent, commission which they charged the unfortunate victims of their benevolent intervention. Finding that I could not help myself, I ordered the delivery of two of those whose agreements I held on Saturday night last. They only had six instead of forty-eight hours' notice, but they were punctually brought to Mdme. Tussaud's at seven o'clock. Mdmes. X. and Z. were both in attendance, and at first insisted upon accompanying their charges to the place of seduction. This, however, for obvious reasons I would not permit, but I had to pay another pound a head before I could get the girls out of their clutches. My friend drove off rapidly in a cab in an opposite direction to the house in which I awaited them, and then doubled back when the procuresses were out of sight. They stipulated, however, that they had to be returned to Mdme. Tussaud's at nine o'clock. The two virgins, both certificated, were among the older girls. One, Bessie, the cook, had been destined for Dr. —. who takes three maids a fortnight. He was out of town, however, and she was brought on to me, to be handed over to an imaginary friend, to whom I was supposed to have resold her. She was eighteen years old. Her father was dead. Her mother was given to drink, and she was in a good situation as under-cook at a first-class hotel. She came perfectly prepared to be seduced, apparently believing it was the proper thing to do, although her ideas were somewhat hazy. I told her before I could take the responsibility of handing her over to my friend I wished to be quite sure, first, that she knew what she was going to experience, and, secondly, that she had calculated the consequences. "I suppose I must go through with it now," she said, "whatever it is." "Oh, no," I replied; "that would be the case in most places; but here you have only to say you would rather not, and you are free to go at once." In conversation I found that the idea of being seduced never occurred to her until a month or two before, when it was proposed by Miss X— as a thing every one did, and a convenient method of raising a little ready money. At first she was indignant and somewhat frightened; but an old school friend who had gone through the ordeal assured her that it was not so very dreadful, and the procuress, to use her own phrase, "so poisoned her mind that she felt she must go through with it," and she consented. She was to have £2. 10s. as her share, the rest would go to the firm. She did not mind the pain, and she would chance the baby, for Miss X. had told her that girls never had babies the first time. She knew it was wrong, her mother would not like it, and if she had a baby she would either get it put away or she would drown herself. But, on the whole, except for one trivial detail, she thought she would prefer to be seduced. "There are very few virtuous girls about now, they say," was the remark by which she apparently soothed her conscience. But the triviality appearing to weigh with her, I sent her into another room to a lady friend, and turned my attention to the second maid, who had been waiting below.

She was a nice, simple, and affectionate girl of sixteen, very different from the other, but even more utterly incapable of understanding the consequences of her act. Her father is "afflicted"–that is, touched in his wits; her mother is a charwoman. She herself works at some kind of millinery, for which she receives 5s. a week. Until a month or two ago she had attended Sunday school, and to all appearance she was a girl decidedly above the average. She was to have £4, of which the firm were to have £2. The poor child was nervous and timid, and it was touching to see the way in which she bit her lips to restrain her tears. I talked to her as kindly as possible, and endeavoured to deter her from taking the fatal step, by setting forth the possible consequences that might follow. She was very frank and I believe perfectly straightforward and sincere. The one thing she dreaded about being seduced was having to be undressed. Poor child, it was the only thing she could realized Her lips quivered and her eyes filled with tears as she pleaded to be allowed to escape that ordeal. What being seduced meant beyond the formula that she would "lose her maid" she had not the remotest idea. When I asked her what she would do if she had a baby, she started, and then said, "But having a baby doesn't come of being seduced, does it? I had no idea of that." "Of course it does," I replied; "they ought to have told you so." "But they did not," she said; "indeed, they said babies never came from a first seduction."

Nevertheless, to my astonishment, the child persisted that she was ready to be seduced. "We are very poor," she said. "Mother does not know anything of this: she will think a lady friend of Miss Z.'s has given me the money; but she does need it so much." "But," I said, "it is only £2." "Yes," she said, "but I would not like to disappoint Miss Z., who was also to have £2." By questioning I found out that the artful procuress had for months past been actually advancing money to the poor girl and her mother when they were in distress, in order to get hold of her when the time came! She persisted that Miss Z. had been such a good friend of hers; she wanted to get her something. She would not disappoint her for anything. "How much do you think she has given you first and last?" "About 10s. I should think, but she gave mother much more." "How much more?" "Perhaps 20s. would cover it." "That is to say, that for a year past Miss Z. has been giving you a shilling here and a shilling there; and why? Listen to me. She has already got £3 from me for you, and you will give her £2– that is to say, she will make £5 out of you in return for 30s., and in the meantime she will have sold you to destruction." "Oh, but Miss Z. is so kind!" Poor, trusting little thing, what damnable art the procuress must have used to attach her victim to her in this fashion! But the girl was quite incapable of forming any calculation as to the consequences of her own action. This will appear from the following conversation. "Now," said I, "if you are seduced you will get £2 for yourself; but you will lose your maidenhood; you will do wrong, your character will be gone, and you may have a baby which it will cost all your wages to keep. Now I will give you £1 if you will not be seduced; which will you have?" "Please sir," she said, "I will be seduced." "And face the pain, and the wrong-doing, and the shame, and the possible ruin and ending your days on the streets, all for the difference of one pound?" "Yes, sir," and she burst into tears, "we are so poor." Could any proof be more conclusive as to the absolute inability of this girl of sixteen to form an estimate of the value of the only commodity with which the law considers her amply able to deal the day after she is thirteen?

PART III. THE MAIDEN TRIBUTE OF MODERN BABYLON

(July 8)

The advocates of the Criminal Law Amendment Bill are constantly met by two mutually destructive assertions. On one side it is declared that the raising of the age of consent is entirely useless, because there are any number of young prostitutes on the streets under the legal age of thirteen, while, on the other, it is asserted as positively that juvenile prostitution below the age of fifteen has practically ceased to exist. Both assertions are entirely false.

There are not many children under thirteen plying for hire on the streets, and there are any number to be had between the ages of thirteen and sixteen. There are children, many children, who are ruined before they are thirteen; but the crime is one phase of the incest which, as the Report of the Dwellings Commission shows, is inseparable from overcrowding. But the number who are on the streets is small. Notwithstanding the most lavish offers of money, I completely failed to secure a single prostitute under thirteen. I have been repeatedly promised children under twelve, but they either never appeared or when produced admitted that they were over thirteen. I have no doubt that I could discover in time a dozen or more girls of eleven or twelve who are leading immoral lives, but they are very difficult to find, as the boys of the same age who pursue the same dreadful calling. This direct evidence is by no means all that is available to show the deterrent effect of raising the age of consent. The Rescue Society, of Finsbury-pavement, which has an experience of thirty-one years, has kept for twenty-five years a record of the ages at which those whom they have rescued lost their character.

The following are the numbers of the rescued who were seduced at the ages of twelve and thirteen for 1862 to 1875, when the close time was raised to thirteen–33, 55, 65, 107, 102, 103, 77, 60, 78, 62, 40, 43, 30: total, 855, or 66 per annum between the ages of twelve and thirteen. From 1875 to 1883 the figures are as follows: 22, 24, 19, 20, 16, 14, 15, 10, 7; total, 147; average, 16 per annum. Allowance must be made for the fact that the total number rescued in 1883 was only half that rescued in 1867, but even then the number of children seduced at twelve and thirteen would have been reduced by one-half owing to the raising of the age. All those who have the best means of knowing how the law would work, gaol chaplains and the rest, are strongly in favour of extending the close time. The preventive operation of the law is much more effective than I anticipated, for it is almost the sole barrier against a constantly increasing appetite for the immature of both sexes. That this infernal taste prevails is unfortunately beyond all gainsaying, and for proof we need go no further than the reports of the numerous refuges and homes for children which have been opened of late years in the neighbourhood of London. But in the ordinary market the supply is limited to girls who are over thirteen.

THE RUIN OF THE VERY YOUNG

There is fortunately no need to dwell upon this revolting phrase of criminality, for it is recognized by the law, and the criminals when caught are soundly punished. My object throughout has been to indicate crimes virtually encouraged by the law; but it is necessary to refer to cases where even penal servitude has not deterred men from the perpetration of this most ruthless of outrages, in order to show the need for strengthening the barrier which alone stands between infants and the brutal lust of dissolute men. Here, for example, is a portrait of a tiny little mite in the care of a rescue officer of our excellent Society for the Protection of Children. Her name is Annie Bryant, and she is now just five years old. Yet that baby girl has been the victim of rape. She was enticed together with a companion into a house in the New Cut on May 28, and forcibly outraged, first by a young man named William Hemmings, and then by a fellow-lodger. The offence was completed, and the poor little child received internal injuries from which it is doubtful whether she will ever entirely recover. The scoundrel is now doing two years penal servitude, but his accomplice escaped. A penny cake was the lure which enticed the baby to her ruin. As I nursed her on my knee, and made her quite happy with a sixpence, the matron of the refuge where the little waif was sheltered told how every night before the baby girl went to sleep she would shudder and cry, and whisper in her ear. And not until the poor child was solemnly assured and reassured that the door was fast, and that no "bad man" could possibly get in, would she dare to go to sleep. Every night it was the same, and when I saw her it was nearly three weeks since her evil fate had befallen her!

This instance of a child of such tender years being subjected to outrage is not an isolated one. A girl of eighteen who is now walking Regent-street had her little sister of five violated by a "gentleman" whom she had brought home. She had left the room for a few minutes, and he took advantage of her absence to ruin the poor child, who was sleeping peacefully in another corner of the room. The man in this case escaped unpunished. As a rule the children who are sent to homes as " fallen" at the age of ten, eleven, and twelve, are children of prostitutes, bred to the business, and broken in prematurely to their dreadful calling. There are children" of five in homes now who, although they have not technically fallen, are little better than animals possessed by an unclean spirit, for the law of heredity is as terribly true in the brothel as elsewhere. One child in St. Cyprian's was turned out on to the streets by her mother to earn a living when ten. At St Mary's Home they do not receive any children over sixteen. Sister Emma has at present more than fifty children in her home in Hants. She receives none under twelve. In only four cases was the man punished. The proportion of victims among the protected is, however, comparatively small to those who have passed the fatal age of thirteen. If Mr. Hastings, who would fix the age of consent at ten, or Mr. Warton, who was in favour of even a lower age than ten, was allowed to have his way, we should probably have to start homes to accommodate infants of four, five, and six who had been ruined "by their own consent." What blasphemy!

THE CHILD PROSTITUTE

It has been computed, says the report of a Hampshire Home, that there are no less than 10,000 little girls living in sin in Christian England. I do not know how far that is correct, but there is no doubt as to the existence of a vast and increasing mass of juvenile prostitution. The Report of the Lords' Committee in 1882 says:–

The evidence before the Committee proves beyond doubt that juvenile prostitution from an almost incredibly early age is increasing to an appalling extent In England, and especially in London. They are unable, adequately to Express their tense of the magnitude, both in amoral and physical point of view, of the evil thus brought to light, and of the necessity for taking vigorous measures to cope with it.

Unfortunately the evil, instead of being coped with, is in the opinion of the chaplains of our gaols rather on the increase than otherwise. The victims are for the most part thirteen, fourteen, and fifteen years old.

At West end houses of the better sort, that is to say, houses where nothing can be done without a preliminary expenditure of a sovereign in a bottle of champagne, and where the ordinary fee, without allowing for tips and wine, is £5, they are very timid in purveying very young girls. I should have had much less difficulty in establishing the fact but for the awe that has fallen upon the unholy sisterhood since the chief among them all was compiled to plead guilty in order to save her clients from exposure. Houses French, Spanish, and English in fashionable localities where, according to current report, you might either meet a Cabinet Minister or be supplied with any number of little children, are now indignant at any application by a stranger for the accommodation which they only extend to their old clients. But at one villa in the north of London I found through the assistance of a friend a lovely child between fourteen and fifteen, tall for her age, but singularly attractive in her childish innocence. At first the keeper strenuously denied that they had any such article in the house, but on mentioning who had directed us to her place, the fact was admitted and an appointment was arranged.

There was another girl in the house— a brazen-faced harlot, whose flaunting vice served as a foil to set off the childlike, spirituelle beauty of the other's baby face. It was cruel to see the poor wee features, not much larger than those of a doll, of the delicately nurtured girl, as she came into the room with her fur mantle wrapped closely round her, and timidly asked me if I would take some wine. Poor child, she had been out driving to the Inventories that morning, and was somewhat tired and still. It seemed a profanation to touch her, she was so young and so baby-like. There she was, turned over to the first comer that would pay, but still to all appearance so modest, the maiden bloom not altogether having faded off her childish cheeks, and her pathetic eyes, where still lingered the timid glance of a frightened fawn. I felt like one of the damned. "She saw old gentlemen," she said, "almost exclusively. Sometimes it was rather bad, but she liked the life," she said, timidly trying to face the grim inexorable, "and the wine, she was so fond of that," although her glass stood untasted before her. Poor thing! When I left the house as a guilty thing, shrinking away abashed from before the presence of the child with her baby eyes, I said to the keeper who let me out, "She is too good for her trade, poor thing." "Wait a bit," said the woman, with a leer. "She is very young —only turned fourteen, and has just come out, you know. Come again in a couple of months, and you will see a great change." A great change, indeed. Would to God she died before that! And she was but one.

HOW CRIMINALS ARE SHIELDED BY THE LAW

This frightful development of fantastic vice is directly encouraged by the law, which marks off all girls over thirteen as fair game for men. It is only in the spring of this year that a man was sentenced to a term of imprisonment for indecent assault upon a child. It was shown in evidence that he had violated more than a dozen children just over thirteen, whom he had enticed into backyards by promises of sweetmeats, but though they did not know what he was doing until they felt the pain, they were over age, and so he escaped scot free, until one day he was fortunately caught with a child under thirteen, and was promptly punished. The Rev. J. Horsley, the chaplain at Clerkenwell, stated last year:–

There is a monster now walking about who acts as clerk in a highly respectable establishment He is fifty years of age. For years it has been his villainous amusement to decoy and ruin children. A very short time ago sixteen cases were proved against him before a magistrate on the Surrey side of the river. The children were all fearfully injured, possibly for life. Fourteen of the girls were thirteen years old, and were therefore beyond the protected age, and it could not be proved that they were not consenting parties. The wife of the scoundrel told the officer who had the case in charge that it was her opinion that her husband ought to be burned. Yet by the English law we cannot touch this monster of depravity, or so much as inflict a small fine on him.

A CLOSE TIME FOR GIRLS

Before the 14th of August it is a crime to shoot a grouse, lest an immature cheeper should not yet have a fair chance to fly. The sports-man who wishes to follow the partridge through the stubbles must wait till September 1, and the close time for pheasants is even later.

Admitting that women are as fair game as grouse and partridges, why not let us have a close time for bipeds in petticoats as well as for bipeds In feathers? At present that close time is absurdly low. The day after a girl has completed her thirteenth year she is perfectly free to dispose of her person to the first purchaser. A bag of sweets, a fine feather, a good dinner, or a treat to the theatre are sufficient to induce her to part with that which may be lost in an hour, but can never be recovered. This is too bad. It does not give the girls a fair chance. The close time ought to be extended until they have at least attained physical maturity. That surely is not putting the matter on too sentimental grounds. Fish out of season are not fit to be eaten. Girls who have not reached the age of puberty are not fit even to be seduced. The law ought at least to be as strict about a live child as about a dead salmon.

Now, what is the age of puberty with English girls? A medical man, Dr. Lowndes, who was recommended to me by Mr. Cavendish Bentinck as a leading surgeon of Liverpool and a great supporter of the C. D. Acts, says:– "I should like to tell you why so many members of the medical profession, including myself, would wish to see an extension of the age in females under which it should be a misdemeanour for any male to have carnal knowledge. It is because so few girls are really aptae-viro, physically and medically, till long after thirteen years of age. My colleague has a girl in the Lock Hospital who is nineteen years old, has been a prostitute for some time, and yet has only just attained puberty. All the cases of abnormal precocity we have heard of, such as mothers at eleven, andc., are very exceptional, and it seems to me that carnal knowledge of any female under puberty is a cruel outrage." That "cruel outrage" is not forbidden by the law. It can be perpetrated and is perpetrated constantly, with perfect impunity to the man, with horrible consequences to the girl. It is also the fact that such children are far more likely to transmit disease than a full-grown woman. Scientifically, therefore, the close time should be extended until the woman has at least completed sixteen years of life. The recommendation of the Lords' Committee was that the close time should last for sixteen years. That was the age accepted by the House of Lords in two successive years, and that is the age which the late Home Secretary promised to insert in the present bill, which legalizes consent when the girl is fifteen years old and a day.

JUVENILE PROSTITUTION IN THE EAST AND WEST

In the East-end of London vice is much more natural than in the West I have made the casual acquaintance of some score of the youngest prostitutes whom the West-end experts could procure. The Congregational Union gave a supper to some seventy young prostitutes in Miss Steer's Bridge of Hope. So far as I could judge, there are very few much under fifteen. Down Ratcliff-highway, and in the parts adjacent, there are plenty at about fifteen or sixteen, but the taste for extreme youth does not seem to have developed in the crowded East. Here and there there are cases, and there are vast strata where the children cohabit from preposterously early years, but that is quite distinct from prostitution. In the most fashionable houses of ill fame, such as Mrs. Jefferies's, Mrs. B — 's, J —— 's, and others, any stranger ordering young children of very tender age would be looked at askance. These things are only done for old customers. In the Edgware-road, two keepers of houses of accommodation were found virtuous enough to refuse admittance to a girl of fourteen and her companion, but they were watched by a vigilance committee. In one of the fashionable houses in Park-lane, where inquiry was made whether any objection would be made to receiving a very, very young girl who was expected with an old gentleman, the reply was: "Of course not. Do you think we insist on the production of the baptismal register of all the ladies who visit us?" I was assured I might bring whom I pleased, as many as I pleased, and no questions would be asked.

In and about the Quadrant and Regent-street I have taken or caused to be taken repeatedly to houses of accommodation young girls from thirteen and upwards who have been picked up on the streets: no objection was ever raised by the keepers. These children were in no sense mature. They usually professed to be fifteen, but did not look thirteen; they usually go in couples, piding their earnings, and as a rule the child is accompanied by a friend who is older than herself. Their story is pretty much the same all round. They were poor, work was bad, every crust they ate at home was grudged, they stopped out all night with some "gay" friend of the female sex, and they went the way of all the rest. Occasionally they say that a gentleman took them to his chambers and ruined them, for consideration received. More of them are patronized by old men, and early initiated into the worst forms of elaborate vice. Many of them are at work in the day, and most of them have to be at home at night at ten or eleven. They have the entry to coffee shops and other houses of call. It was not necessary to prosecute this branch of the subject to any great length. Lest any doubt should still prevail as to the reality of this description of the traffic, I may say that I have at this moment an agreement with the keeper of one of the houses near Regent-street to the effect that she will have ready in her house, within a few hours of receipt of a line from me, a girl under fourteen. I have only tested it once, but I should not have the least hesitation in trusting her to fulfil it again.

THE RUIN OF THE YOUNG LIFE. – "THE DEMON CHILD"

"These young girls," says the Report of the Rescue Society for 1883, are more difficult to deal with than women, because they are made familiar with sin while so young that the modesty that is so natural to a woman they never attain." The matron of a Lock Hospital, a good, kindly, motherly soul, assured me that, according to their painful but almost invariable experience, they found that the innocent girl once outraged seemed to suffer a lasting blight of the moral sense. They never came to any good: the foul passion from the man seemed to enter into the helpless victim of his lust, and she never again regained her pristine purity of soul. The physical consequences are often terrible. Here is the story of a child-prostitute who, at the age of eleven, had for two years been earning her living by vice in the East-end. My informant says:–

Emily.–Short of her age, broad and stout, with a pleasant face with varying expression; sometimes a fearfully old look, and sometimes with the face of childhood; she told me she had never had a toy in her life or ever been in a garden. I found her to be fearfully diseased and sent her to the Lock Hospital. She was there about six weeks. Returned looking fat and well, but odd in her ways, her mind fearfully fouled by the life she had led, and which

she liked to talk about. Some one called her "the Demon Child," and it was an apt name for her. Offended, she would scream as if she was being murdered if no one touched her; only a look from some would set her off: no one seemed able to pacify her; if possible she would get away from everybody and lie down close to a large bed of mignonette, and put her head amongst it and become calm, "Just an excuse for idleness and wickedness," some would say, but I saw her do it dozens of times, and gave directions that she should not be prevented from going into the garden, she was such a child. One day I saw her as usual tear shrieking along the broad walk and away to the path by the greenhouse, sit down under an apple tree, and burying her head in thick grass bloom, subside from shrill screams to sobs and low cries and then to a perfect calm, so I went down and said, "Why do you always run to this corner, little one; does the sweet mignonette do you good, and cure you of being naughty?" "It's the devil makes me so bad," she answered in a moment, "and I think the nice smell sends him away; and down went her head again.

Strange that the fragrance of the mignonette should calm the shattered nerves of the demon child, who had probably never before enjoyed the smell of a flower. Alternate imbecility and wild screaming are too common among the child victims of vice. Well may they scream—far worse their lot than the little slaves of the loom of whom Mrs. Browning says :—

Well may those children weep before you,
They are weary ere they ran;
They have never seen the sunshine, nor the glory
Which is brighter than the sun.
They know the grief of man, but not the wisdom;
They sink in man's despair without its calm;
Are slaves without the liberty in Christdom,
Are martyrs, by the pang without the palm—
Are worn, as if with age, yet unretrievingly
No dear remembrance keep
Are orphans of the earthly love and heavenly.
Let them weep! let them weep!

HOW THE LAW FACILITATES ABDUCTION

It is sometimes said that these children ought to be looked after by their parents, but those who resort to that argument forget that the law plays into the hands of the abductor. Suppose a child of thirteen, either in a fit of temper or enticed by the bribes of a procuress, once gets within the precincts of a brothel, what is the parent to do? The brothel-keeper has only to keep the door locked to defy the father. If she had stolen a doll he could have got a search warrant for stolen property, but as it is only his daughter he can do nothing. It is true that there is a mode of procedure by habeas corpus, but that is so cumbrous and so costly that it is practically unavailable for the poor. Counsel's opinion was recently taken by the abductor of a boy as to what steps could be taken to prevent the father obtaining possession of his son. The answer was as follows:– Refuse father admittance. You can keep the boy until Habeas Corpus is obtained. At the very earliest this can not be secured until after twenty-four hours at least. The hearing of the case to show cause will wait about a week for a turn. The costs are uncertain, from £30 to £50.

What is the use of a remedy which at the earliest cannot be brought into operation in less than twenty-four hours, even if it could be had for nothing? A girl may be ruined in ten minutes. By habeas corpus a father has a means of gaining his end, but he could no more raise the £50 needed than he could fly. A remedy that involves a preliminary expenditure of £50, and can then only get into action in a week, is virtually non-existent for the poor.

Take another case. In Hull last August a man kept a child's brothel, locally known as "the Infant School." He kept no fewer than fourteen children there, the eldest only fifteen, and some as young as twelve. The mothers had gone to the house to try and claim their children, and had been driven off by the prisoner with the most horrible abuse, and had no power to get the children away or even to see them. Fortunately, the old reprobate had sold drink without a licence. For this offence, and not for his stealing children, the police broke into his house and secured his conviction. By law abduction is no offence unless the girl is in the custody of her father at the time of her abduction.

How easy it is for a man to seduce a child with impunity the following record taken from the report of a case heard in Hammersmith police-court last March will show:–

Walter Franklin, who lived in North-avenue, Fulham, was summoned for unlawfully taking Annie Summers, an unmarried girl, under the age of sixteen, out of the possession of her master, and against the will of her father. Mr. Gregory said he appeared on behalf of the Society for the Protection of Young Girls to support the summons. The girl, who was fourteen, was in service, and met the defendant while on her way to her father to obtain a change of linen. He invited her to his house, where he kept her all night, and turned her out in the morning. She was found by her father in Chelsea. Mr. Sheil referred to the case of "Queen and Miller," and thought no charge had been disclosed, as she was not in the custody of her father. The case fell in with the decision in "Queen and Miller." In that case it was the converse. The girl had left her father, and was on the way to her mistress. Mr. Gregory: You think she was not in the custody of either? Mr. Sheil replied in the Affirmative. The summons was then withdrawn.

ENTRAPPING IRISH GIRLS

I have already spoken of procuring children and silly London girls. Of a deeper shade of criminality is the system of trapping innocent girls by inveigling them into houses of ill-fame which are represented as respectable lodging-houses. A few years ago, when great numbers of Irish girls used to arrive in the Thames, they formed a constant source of revenue to the brothel keepers of Ratcliffe-highway. The modus operandi was very simple. The moment the steamer touched the landing it was hoarded by men retained by the brothel keepers to bring girls home. Sometimes they accosted the girl, saying that if she wanted a cheap respectable lodging they could take her to exactly the kind of place she wanted. More frequently they seized her box and marched off with it, assuring her that they were taking it to the place where she had to stop. The Irish girl, being innocent and inexperienced, setting foot for the first time in a foreign city, without friends and not knowing where to go, followed the porter, and was soon safely housed A highly respectable Irish girl in the service of one of my friends had the utmost difficulty in extricating her box from the grasp of one of these harpies. As, however, it was the second visit, and as she knew the address where a situation awaited her, she succeeded in compelling him to leave her box, and let her go to the place. A less experienced girl, who had no address to which to go, would have fallen an easy prey. When the girl is once within the brothel she is about as helpless as a sparrow when caught by the falling brick of the schoolboy's trap. The method of her gaoler is very simple. The object being in all cases purely mercenary, the first thing is to strip her of all her scanty store of money. This is done not by theft, but by running up a bill for board and lodgings, and to this end every impediment is placed in the way of finding her a situation. The mere fact of her lodging in such a house stands in the way of her success, even without the many simple but effective expedients which can be employed to prevent her engagement.

The next thing is to get her into debt, and this also is easily accomplished by the same means. All the time the bill is running up, the girl is insidiously tempted. She is plied with drink, significant hints are dropped as to the money she might make if she would "do as the others do;" possibly a lover is found for her, no stone is left unturned to sap her virtue. If she is obdurate to the last, two things happen. Her box containing all her worldly goods is seized and she is turned penniless into the street, late at night, without a friend or acquaintance in the whole world, and with dire threats of being handed over to the police for not paying her bill. What is she to do? A country girl of seventeen or eighteen without a penny in her pocket in Ratcliff-highway at midnight is marked down for destruction. The very contemplation of such a position is sufficient to coerce the girl, if not into complying at least into considering her captors' proposals. Forlorn and desperate, she is tempted to drink, some snuff is put in her beer, she becomes unconscious, and when she wakes with a splitting headache in the morning, the girl is lost. This is no fancy picture. Priests and harlots both agree that it is the simple truth. Cardinal Manning assured me that so terrible was the havoc among these immigrants that one notorious procuress in those parts boasted that no fewer than 1,600 girls had passed through her hands. That, however, was some years ago. The Irish immigration has almost ceased.

The influx of Irish immigration is comparatively small, but some girls still arrive in London from Liverpool. The snaring of these girls is accomplished with more art than by the lassoing method that used to prevail in Ratcliff-highway. One of the most ingenious, but most diabolical methods of capture is that which consists in employing a woman dressed as a Sister of Merry as a lure. This I have been assured by ladies actively engaged in work among the poor is sometimes adopted with great success. The Irish Catholic girl arriving at Euston is accosted by what appears to be a Sister or Mercy. She is told that the good Lady Superior has sent her to meet poor Catholic girls to take them to good lodgings, where she can look about for a place. The girl naturally follows her guide, and after a rapid ride in a closed cab through a maze of streets she is landed in a house of ill fame. After she is shown to her bedroom the Sister of Mercy disappears, and the field is cleared for her ruin. The girl has no idea where she is. Every one is kind to her. The procuress wins her confidence. Perhaps a situation is found for her in another house belonging to the same management, for some broth-keepers have several houses. Drink is constantly placed in her way; she is taken to the theatre and dances. Some night, when worn out and half intoxicated, her bedroom door is opened – for there are doors which when locked inside will open by pressure from without – and her ruin is accomplished. After that all is easy – except the return to a moral life. Vestigia nulla retrorsum.

DECOY GIRLS AND THEIR ARTS

It is by no means only Irish girls who are the prey of the procuress. English and Scotch are picked up with even greater facility. There are decoy girls in every great thoroughfare – agents of the procuress in almost every railway station. Children as they go to and from day school and Sunday school are noted by the keen eye of the professional decoy–waited for and watched until the time has come for running them down. "Baker-street station," said a female missionary," is regularly haunted by an old decoy, who entices little children to a place in Milton-street. Watch has been kept for weeks at a time, but she is wary, and when the watch is on the decoy goes elsewhere. As soon as the watch is removed we hear from children whom she has tempted that she is back at her old haunts." Most respectable little girls of the middle class are sometimes accosted when looking into shop windows by pleasant-spoken, well-dressed ladies, who offer to buy anything they take a fancy to in order to win their confidence and get them away.

One fine child of fourteen in the Brompton-road was promised by "such a nice little lady" rides on her beautiful quiet pony as often as she liked, if she would only go home with her. The thing is not done impromptu. It is a carefully organized system, worked by professionals, whose earnings are large and whose risk is small. Of 3,000 cases of which particulars have been taken in Millbank nearly 900, or about 30 per cent, attributed their ruin to decoy girls. When once a child is enticed away she is often too much ashamed to go back, and even if she wished, good care is taken to keep her in the toils. As for tracing her, a needle in a bottle of hay is as easily found as a child among the four millions of London. Some years ago an old procuress enticed away the daughter of a city missionary. The girl disappeared for six months. The police were put on the alert. Handbills were printed and circulated broadcast. Everything was done to track the girl, and everything was done in vain. Her mother almost lost her reason, and all hope was abandoned when the girl turned up one day at a refuge. It was then discovered that she had never been out of London, that at one time she had been in the workhouse, and that she never had made any attempt at keeping out of view. She was simply lost in the Babylonian maze.

RUINING COUNTRY GIRLS

The country girl offers an almost unresisting quarry. Term time, when young girls come up to town with their boxes to seek situations, is the great battue season of the procuress. To such a pass has it come that when a member of the Girls' Friendly Society comes to town to a situation, the society deems it indispensable to send some one to meet her to see that she does not fall into bad hands. In dealing with English girls the woman is sometimes dressed as a deaconess instead of a sister of mercy. "It makes one's heart bleed," said a porter at one of the Northern railway stations," to see these poor girls snapped up by these bad women." Even if they escape from the railway station they are often trapped in the street. Here is a case which came under the personal knowledge of the chaplain at Westminster prison, A country girl arrived by the Great Northern Railway at King's Cross. She put her boxes in the left-luggage room and went out, as thousands have done before her, to see what London looked like, and to inquire her way about.

After some little time, being hungry and tired, she asked an apparently respectable woman where she could get something to eat. The woman took her to a refreshment house, where they had some food. The drink was apparently drugged, for the girl remembered nothing until several hours after, when she came to consciousness in a police cell. She had been found lying, apparently drunk, in the street, and had been run in. On recovering herself she found that her purse had been taken, the tickets for her luggage carried off, most of her underclothing had been taken away, and that she was very sore and scratched about the thighs. Apparently disturbed before they were able to proceed to the last extremity, the criminals had hurriedly dressed her in a few clothes and deposited her in the street, where she was found still unconscious by the policeman. On inquiry at the Left Luggage Office, it was found that her boxes had been removed by some one who had produced the ticket, but who he was no one has ever been able to discover any trace. The girl was proved to be very respectable. A place was found for her, and she has done well ever since. Mr. Merrick, who saw her repeatedly and questioned her closely, has no doubt whatever that she gave a truthful statement of what actually took place, and but for an accident she would have been outraged as well as robbed. Others less lucky are now on the streets; but their stories of course are easily dismissed.

Here is another case, the accuracy of which is vouched for by a lady engaged in rescue work at Pimlico. A young girl, aged sixteen or seventeen, coming from the country on a visit to her uncle, a wealthy tradesman, was looking after her boxes at the railway station, when a woman, addressing her by her name, asked her where she was going. "To my uncle, who lives at ——." The woman replied, "I have been sent to fetch you." She took the girl in a cab and landed her in a brothel, from which she was not rescued for some time. The woman had read the girl's name in the address on her boxes.

These malpractices are by no means confined to London. Here is a tale for the truth of which Mr. Charrington is ready to vouch:—

A young lady applied to the proprietor of a provincial music-hall for an engagement, and as the photograph showed a very pretty girl of some eighteen Summers, a favourable reply was sent, and respectable (?) lodgings were procured for her. He allowed her to sing one night, but ere the second night was passed he had drugged her, seduced her, and communicated to her a foul and loathsome disease. My friend (who told me her story) found her literally rotting on some straw in an outhouse where the proprietor had left her to starve. At first he thought there was no hope of recovery, but her life was saved, although her beauty and her eyesight were both gone.

In a report on the social condition of Edinburgh drawn up by Mr. Fairbairn, a city missionary in 1883, he says:—

Some houses which are nominally temperance hotels are in reality brothels (they take the name of temperance hotels because they are thus open to receive people, and at the same time escape police supervision, having no licence). Into these places girls are entrapped as servants, and drugged or made drunk, and then seduced, and tempted to abandon themselves to prostitution. In two such cases known to the missionary, the keepers have been sent to prison. At a famous brothel at Liverpool, country girls were frequently trapped—excursionists and cheap trippers being the favourite prey.

IMPRISONED IN BROTHELS

It is easy enough to get into a brothel, it is by no means easy to get out. Apart from the dress houses, where women are practically prisoners, forbidden to cross the doorstep and chained to the house by debt, cases are constantly occurring in which girls find themselves under lock and key. Every now and then fervid Protestantism lashes itself into wild fury over the alleged abduction of some girl who is believed to have been spirited away from convent to convent. These abductions and imprisonments are constantly going on in the service of vice, but no one pays any heed. The labyrinth of London, like that of Crete, has many chambers and underground passages; the clue that leads to the entrance is easily broken. Here, for instance, is one case in which a girl who is now in a respectable situation was imprisoned until her ruin was effected.

K. S., a nursemaid, under fifteen, was once asked to take tea by a woman whose acquaintance she had made. She entered and was not allowed to go out. She was detained in the house, but kindly treated. One night she was drugged, rendered unconscious, and when in that condition she was ruined, it was said, by a nobleman. He kept her there for some months, when at last she succeeded in making her escape. The house is in a street near the Marble Arch, kept by Miss—, who pretended to keep a dyer's shop. The girl was sent to Cheshire from the Lock Hospital, and is now doing well.

Here is another case reported by a Westminster Rescue Home:–

Fanny F., fifteen, was imprisoned in the brothel. Her father was denied all access to the house. He was in great trouble, but at last he got her out by help of other girl inmates, who had heard of the father's grief.

Even when they do escape the brothel keeper seizes possession of their things. The case of Esther Prausner, a Polish girl, which came before the Thames police court at the end of June, is–

She came to England from Germany a few months since, for the purpose of getting a livelihood. After she had been over here a few weeks she was persuaded to live at Poplar in a house of ill fame, and the unfortunate girl while there was compelled to lead an immoral life. At last she declined to stay any longer in the house, and left. When she demanded her box, containing all her things, and also those of a young man whom she intended to marry, the landlady refused to give them up, saying that she should not have them at all. The girl had paid not only the rent for all the time she lived in the house but also a week's rent in advance in lieu of notice to quit. Still her box was not given up. She asked the magistrate's advice as to what she should do to recover her property. Mr. Lushington having directed one of the warrant officers to go to the house and try and obtain the box, was informed, later on in the day, that the woman would not give it up. He then directed a summons, free of charge, to be issued against the person referred to for illegally detaining the things. The young girl, who was nineteen, and appeared in great distress, then withdrew.

A case which came more immediately under my personal knowledge was one which occurred only last year in St. John's-wood. Although I have not been able to see the girl herself I have received from two trustworthy and independent sources narratives of her adventure which are substantially identical. It is as follows:–

Alice B., a Devonshire girl of twenty years of age, came to London to service on the death of her father. She was seduced when in service by a doctor who lodged in the house; but after he left she kept company with an apparently respectable young man. She was engaged to be married, and all seemed to be going well, when one Sunday afternoooon (sic), as they were enjoying their Sunday walk, he proposed to call and see his aunt, who lived, he said, at No. – Queen's-road, St. John's Wood. This house, local rumour asserts, is a fashionable brothel, patronized among others by at least one Prince and one Cabinet Minister. Of that she knew nothing. Together with her sweetheart she entered the house and had tea with his supposed aunt. After tea she was asked if she would not like to wash her hands, and she was taken upstairs to a handsomely furnished bedroom and left alone. She first discovered her situation by hearing the key turn in the lock. For three weeks she was never allowed to leave the room, but was compelled to receive the visits of her first seducer, who seems to have employed her sweetheart to lure her into this den. She implored her captor to release her, but although he took her to the theatre and the opera, dressed her in fine clothes, and talked of marrying her abroad, he never allowed her to escape. When he was not with her she was kept under lock and key. When he was with her, she was a captive under surveillance. This went on for six or seven weeks. The girl was well fed and cared for, and had a maid to wait on her; but she fretted in captivity, dreaming constantly of escape, but being utterly unable to get out of the closely guarded house. At last one morning she was roused by an unusual noise. It was the sweep brushing the chimney. Her door had to be opened to allow him to enter the adjoining room. She rose, dressed herself in her old clothes -which fortunately had not been removed–and fled for her life. She found a little side door at the bottom of the back stairs open, and in a moment she was free, She had neither hat nor bonnet, nor had she a penny she could call her own. Her one thought was to get as far away as possible from the hated house. For three or four days she wandered friendless and helpless about the street, not knowing where to go. The police were kind to her and saved her from insult, but she was nearly starved when by a happy inspiration she made her way to a Salvation Army meeting at Whitechapel, where she fell into good hands. She was passed on to their Home and then to the Rescue Society, by whose agency she found a situation, where she is at the present moment.

It would be painful to discover how many girls are at this moment imprisoned like Alice B. in the brothels of London.

A LONDON MINOTAUR

As in the labyrinth of Crete there was a monster known as the Minotaur who devoured the maidens who were cast into the mazes of that evil place, so in London there is at least one monster who may be said to be an absolute incarnation of brutal lust. The poor maligned brute in the Cretan labyrinth but devoured his tale of seven maids and as many boys every ninth year. Here in London, moving about clad as respectably in broad cloth and fine linen as any bishop, with no foul shape or semblance of brute beast to mark him off from the rest of his fellows, is Dr,——, now retired from his profession and free to devote his fortune and his leisure to the ruin of maids. This is the "gentleman" whose quantum of virgins from his procuresses is three per fortnight–all girls who have not previously been seduced. But his devastating passion sinks into insignificance compared with that of Mr. ——, another wealthy man, whose whole life is dedicated to the gratification of lust. During my investigations in the subterranean realm I was constantly coming across his name. This procuress was getting girls for ——, that woman was beating up maids for ——, this girl was waiting for ——, that house was a noted place of ——'s. I ran across his traces so constantly that I began to make inquiries in the upper world of this redoubtable personage. I soon obtained confirmation of the evidence I had gathered at first hand below as to the reality of the existence of this modern Minotaur, this English Tiberius, whose Caprece is in London.

It is no part of my commission to hold up inpiduals to popular execration, and the name and address of this creature will not appear in these columns. But the fact that he exists ought to be put on record, if only as a striking illustration of the extent to which it is possible for a wealthy man to ruin not merely hundreds but thousands of poor women, It is actually Mr. ——'s boast that he has ruined 3,000 women in his time. He never has anything to do with girls regularly on the streets, but pays liberally for actresses, shop-girls, and the like. Exercise, recreation; everything is subordinated to the supreme end of his life. He has paid his victims, no doubt–never gives a girl less than £5—but it is a question whether the lavish outlay of £3,000 to £5,000 on purchasing the assent of girls to their own dishonour is not a frightful aggravation of the wrong which he has been for some mysterious purpose permitted to inflict on his Kind.

'Tis not vain fabulous,
Though as esteem'd by shallow ignorance,
What the sage poets, taught by the heav'nly muse,
Storied of old, in high immortal verse,
Of dire chimeras and enchanted isles.
And rifted rocks whose entrance leads to Hell;
For such there be, but unbelief is blind.

The blindest unbelief must admit that in this "English gentleman", we have a far more hideous Minotaur than that which Ovid fabled and which Theseus slew.

PART IV. THE MAIDEN TRIBUTE OF MODERN BABYLON

(July 10)

The watchword with which we started, Liberty for Vice, Repression for Crime, is the only safe keynote for the Legislature in dealing with this question. The Criminal Law Amendment Bill, as framed by Sir W. Harcourt, was not so much a bill for raising the age of consent and increasing the stringency of the provisions against procuration and the traffic in English girls as a bill for increasing the arbitrary power of the police in the streets.

No one who has any acquaintance with the enormous variety of the duties which modern civilization imposes upon the police can sympathize with the abuse so ignorantly and uncharitably showered upon the force. The constable is the official upon whom modern society has devolved all the duties of the ancient knight errant. There is no more useful being in the world, and there are few nobler ideals of human activity than the daily life of a really public-spirited, chivalrous policeman. But the majority of policemen, being only mortal, are no more to be trusted with arbitrary power than any other human beings, especially over the other sex. Its possession leads to corruption, and the more that power is increased the more mischief is done. I have no wish to bring any railing accusations against a body of men who are constantly performing the most arduous duties in the public service; but those who think most highly of the force should be most anxious to save it from any increase of a temptation which already seriously impairs both its morale and its efficiency. In this, I am informed, I am expressing not only the unanimous opinion of our

Commission, but also the matured conviction of some of the best authorities in the force.

The power of the police over women in the streets is already ample, not merely for the purposes of maintaining order and for preventing indecency and molestation, but also for the purpose of levying blackmail upon unfortunates.

I have been assured by a chaplain of one of her Majesty's gaols, who perhaps has more opportunities of talking to these women than any other individual in the realm, that there is absolute unanimity in the ranks that if they do not tip the police they get run in. From the highest to the lowest, he informs me, the universal testimony is that you must pay the constable, or you get into trouble. With them it has come to be part of the recognized necessities of their profession. Tipping porters is contrary to the by-laws of the railway companies, yet it is constantly done by passengers; and tipping the police is as constant a practice on the part of the women of the street. Some pay with purse, others with person—many poor wretches with both. There are good policemen who would not touch the money of a harlot or drink with her, much less have anything to do with her otherwise. But there are great numbers who regard these things as the perquisites of their office, and who act on their belief.

The power of a policeman over a girl of the streets, although theoretically very slight, is in reality almost despotic. "If you quarrel with a policeman you are done for," is not far from the truth. The esprit de corps of the force is strong, and both prostitutes and policemen agree in this, that if a girl were once to tip and tell she might just as well leave London at once. She would be harried out of division after division, and never allowed to rest until she was outside the radius of the metropolitan district. If policemen can do that to avenge a breach of faith, it need not be pointed out that they are able materially to affect a girl's position and prospects without absolutely doing anything wrong. They have only to appear inconveniently inquisitive when a bargain is being driven in order to scare off a customer, and at any time, if they choose to be animated by a severe sense of public duty, they can discover evidence sufficient to justify at least a threat of apprehension. A girl's livelihood is in a policeman's hand, and in too many cases he makes the most of his opportunity. To increase by one jot or one tittle the power of the man in uniform over the women who are left unfriended even by their own sex is a crime against liberty and justice, which no impatience at markets of vice, or holy horror at the sight of girls on the streets, ought to be allowed to excuse. If we say that the policeman is constantly tempted to transmute his power into cash, we only say that he is human and that he is poor. But it is too bad to convert the truncheoned custodians of public order into a set of "ponces" in uniform, levying a disgraceful tribute on the fallen maidens of modern Babylon.

AN UNNATURAL ALLIANCE

If the police are constantly in danger of being corrupted by the arbitrary power which they, possess, over prostitutes, the temptation presented by brothels is still more insidious. Every one knows how Mrs. Jefferies tried to tip Minahan, and how his superiors laughed him to scorn because he did not take hush money like the rest. The policeman theoretically has no power over the house of ill fame. But if he chooses he can make it almost impossible for any brothel to do good business. The police, by simple refusal to accept yesterday an interpretation of their duty on which they had acted the previous afternoon, made Northumberland-street impassable and delayed the publication of the Pall Mall Gazette by three hours. Anything more scandalous, that was not openly riotous—for the crowd was very good-humoured—than the scene upon which Lord Aberdeen, the Hon. Auberon Herbert, and many others, looked down upon from our office windows yesterday it would be difficult to conceive. Men were flung bodily through our windows, and had a single door given way the office would have been looted of every paper it contained.

The police for hours gave us no protection, and did little or nothing to secure freedom of egress and of exit to our premises. Whatever may have been the reason it was not until a question was asked in the House of Commons, and a formal complaint lodged at the Home Office, that the police abandoned an interpretation of their duty which for the greater part of the day rendered it impossible for any one to gain access to our premises, or for the ordinary and legitimate business of a newspaper to be carried on. Now, if the police can do this in dealing with an influential journal, with powerful friends in both Houses of Parliament and an immense following in the country, what can they not do in dealing with a brothel-keeper, who is constantly within an ace of breaking the law, even if he does not, as a great many of them do, convert his house into a shebeen? The inevitable result follows. Every brothel becomes more or less a source of revenue to the policemen on the beat. "The police are the brothel-keepers' best friends," said an old keeper to me sententiously. " 'Cos why? They keep things snug. And the brothel-keepers are the police's best friend, 'cos they pay them." "How much did you pay the police?" I asked. "£3 a week year in and year out," he said reflectively, "and mine was only a small house." I have been told that at one famous house in the East-end the police allowance is as much as £500 a year, to say nothing of free quarters when they are wanted, for either the constables or the detectives.

This of course I cannot verify: I can only say that it is a matter-of common repute in the East, and if Sir Richard Cross wishes to know the name and the address of the house for purposes of independent inquiry it is at his service. What is the natural result? An alliance is struck up between the brothel keeper and the constable. A lady skilled in rescue work, and in a position to speak authoritatively, told me that if ever she wished to save a girl from a bad house in the West-end she had to take the greatest care not to allow a whisper of her intention to reach the ears of the police. "If I do." she said, "I nearly always find that the keeper has received a warning, and that the poor girl has been spirited off to some other house." It is better in the East; but in the West, if you want to circumvent the men whose crimes I have been exposing, don't tell the police.

THE BLACK SHEEP OF THE FLOCK

Of course there are police and police. Some the best of men, others very much the reverse. Until Colonel Henderson put his foot down, and gave his superintendents to understand that the roughs were not to be allowed to maltreat the processions of the Salvation Army, the difference between a perfectly peaceful demonstration and a general riot depended almost entirely upon the goodwill or the reverse of the constable on the beat. Hence an enormous responsibility depends upon those who are charged with the maintenance of the high character of the force. Some of the superintendents are excellent men, and many of the inspectors. Others hardly deserve such praise. Mr. Charrington, in a letter received this morning, assures me that when he has gone to try and rescue poor little outraged children the police have done their best to prevent him. On one occasion he declares two policemen actually handed him over to the busies from the brothels to be murdered, saying at the same time they would go round the corner and not see it. "Only a few weeks ago when some good honest policemen did do their duty and protected me by taking into custody a man who assaulted me, they were immediately taken away from the spot and ordered not to go near it, while the scoundrel who did his best to get him murdered was allowed to remain." An ex-officer of long standing assured me that "policemen and soldiers between them ruin more girls than any other class of men in London." From Edinburgh I receive a report from a City missionary that he met with a case in that city where a gentleman saved a girl from a policeman who had threatened to run her in unless he might have his will with her, and, as he adds significantly, for one which we find there may be many. Many of the police are unmarried men, living in barracks as much as soldiers, and are no more fit to be invested with absolute control of the streets, which, after all, are the drawing-room of the poor, than are the Guards. Sometimes there is a thoroughly bad sheep in the flock, and his presence corrupts the rest.

A STARTLING STATEMENT

We have received a horrible statement concerning one officer who was recently in high command in the Metropolitan police—a story so horrible, both in its central fact and still more as to the tyranny which it represents, that we for some time hesitated to publish it. Even now, while promising to communicate to the Home Secretary, in order that the charge may be strictly investigated, the name of the person accused we merely give the tale in outline, so incredible does it appear to us, extracted from a written declaration now before us, which was sworn yesterday before the mayor of Winchester:–

A.B., an officer of high standing in the force, fifteen years ago violently seduced his daughter, who was then sixteen years old. After this intercourse had continued some time she left home, but afterwards falling into distress appealed to her father for help, saying that unless she got relief she would be compelled to apply to the magistrate. He sent a married sister to threaten her with imprisonment if she did anything of the kind. I continue the story in the words of the daughter, who is now a woman of thirty-one years of age, and engaged to be married to a man named Gibbons. "On receiving my statement that I would apply to the magistrate, he, having influence in Scotland-yard, sent two detectives in plain clothes to my lodgings, 1, Caledonian-street, King's-cross. I was alone. One of the men set his back against the door, and they began to intimidate me. They said I was to write a letter to my father and sign it, declaring that my accusation of him was untrue. I refused to write and sign any such letter, as it would be a falsehood. I asked if I could call in Mr. Gibbons, a young man to whom I was engaged to be married, that he might be present as a witness. They then threatened me with ten years' imprisonment and Gibbons with five if I did not write the letter. They had no warrant, but had merely been directed to intimidate me. They brought some note-paper. I had fainted with fear and distress. One of the policemen held me up to the table and composed the letter he wished me to write, and under the threat that they would take me up to prison there and then they held my hand, and forced me to write the letter. I told them, when written, that it was every bit false. I fainted again, and they left me in that condition and went away. I wrote again to my father telling him that although he had sent these detectives to my room to force me to write the letter I'd rather suffer imprisonment to let the truth be known. On the same day that my father received this letter he applied for his pension, and in a short time afterwards he retired from the force on a good pension. We applied to a magistrate in Clerkenwell. He told us he must consult a brother magistrate, and later he informed us that, considering the position of the gentleman who was accused, he would rather not have anything to do with the case. Through the influence of the police reports against Mr. Gibbons were set afloat, and in consequence he lost his situation as a carpenter. Mr. Gibbons has made his statement before a public prosecutor." This statement and other documents relating to the case are, it is said, in the hands of Professor Stuart, M.P. She further avers that Mr. Benjamin Scott, chairman of the London Committee for Stopping the Traffic in English Girls, sent persons to verify my story, and found it to be correct.

Now, if this story be true—and we publish it merely in order to challenge the most searching inquiry, and if possible to secure its immediate contradiction —what a piece of wickedness is here exposed to light! And what security can there be for individual liberty and the protection of female honour if the police in authority on any beat or in any division should be capable of such a crime. But it does not need so startling a piece of evidence as this to show that men, even when helmets are placed on their heads, are not fit to be trusted with what is practically absolute power over women who are even weaker and less protected than the rest of their sex. Hence I regard the excision of the clauses increasing the power of the police over women in the streets as absolutely necessary.

WHAT, THEN, ABOUT THE STATE OF THE STREETS?

Nothing can be more absurdly exaggerated than the usual talk about the scandalous state of the streets. Of course Regent-street at midnight is a grim and soul-saddening sight, and so are one or two other neighbourhoods that might be named. It may be possible to legislate solely for these quarters where vice is congested, by treating them as disorderly places, to be cleared by exceptional powers, only to be brought into exercise by the initiative of two or more residents in the neighbourhood. But we are against exceptional powers, even when initiated by private citizens. If any number of people are really in earnest about abating this scandal, why can they not imitate the example of the people of St. Jude's, King's-cross, and organize a vigilance committee? One or two members of this committee appeared to give evidence of general annoyance, while the police proved the individual acts of solicitation. That cleared the streets at St. Jude's, and it would clear Regent-street. The streets belong to the prostitute as much as to the vestryman, and her right to walk there as long as she behaves herself ought to be defended to the last. Those who take their places if they are dragooned into the slums are certainly no more virtuous than the unreclaimed Magdalens of the streets.

As to the extent of the evil of importunate solicitation, I can bear personal testimony as to the gross exaggeration of the popular notion. I have been a night prowler for weeks. I have gone in different guises to most of the favourite rendezvous of harlots. I have strolled along Ratcliff-highway, and sauntered round and round the Quadrant at midnight. I have haunted St,

James's Park, and twice enjoyed the strange sweetness of summer night by the sides of the Serpentine. I have been at all hours in Leicester-square and the Strand, and have spent the midnight in Mile-end-road and the vicinity of the Tower. Sometimes I was alone; sometimes accompanied by a friend; and the deep and strong impression which I have brought back is one of respect and admiration for the extraordinarily good behaviour of the English girls who pursue this dreadful calling. In the whole of my wanderings I have not been accosted half-a-dozen times, and then I was more to blame than the woman. I was turned out of Hyde Park at midnight in company with a drunken prostitute, but she did not begin the conversation. I have been much more offensively accosted in Parisian boulevards than I have ever been in English park or English street, and on the whole I have brought back from the infernal labyrinth a very deep conviction that if there is one truth in the Bible that is truer than another it is this, that the publicans and harlots are nearer the kingdom of heaven than the scribes and pharisees who are always trying to qualify for a passport to bliss hereafter by driving their unfortunate sisters here to the very real hell of a police despotism.

Only in one respect would I like to see the powers of the police strengthened, and that is in exactly assimilating the law as to man and woman in molestation and solicitation. Why should not the male analogue of a prostitute – the man who habitually and persistently annoys women by solicitation – be subject to the same punishment for annoying girls by offensive overtures as are women who annoy men? It would be a real gain to get rid of one little bit, however small, of the scandalous immorality of having a severe law for the weak and a lax law for the strong.

DO THE POLICE KNOW OF THESE CRIMES

There is one argument that is constantly used, which is utterly worthless. These things could not have happened, it is said, because the police would have found them out long ago. The police knew all about them long ago, but they do not put them down. Here is one fact for the accuracy of which we can vouch from our own personal knowledge. People doubt the existence of the firm of procuresses Mdmes. X. and Z., and their delivery of virgins. What, then, will they say when I tell them, so far from the firm having retired from business owing to the exposure with which all London is ringing, that yesterday, with the street all vocal with the cries of newsboys vending the Pall Mall Gazette's revelations, these worthy women of business delivered over two of the certified virgins to be seduced, and entered into a further contract to supply a girl for export to a foreign brothel? Now, do the police know anything of the transactions of yesterday? If they do not know now, when we have told them all about it, what value is the argument that facts are not facts because the police must have found out all about them long ago if they had been true?

THE POLICE AND THE SECRET COMMISSION

I have often been asked whether, in the course of the six weeks during which our Secret Commission was investigating, any of its members were arrested by the police or in any way incommoded in their apparently criminal transactions by the authorities at Scotland-yard. In no single instance did we experience the slightest inconvenience from the members of the force. Experimental contracts were entered into and executed, maidens were examined and despatched to their destinations, and arrangements made for the supposed perpetration of similar crimes to those which have excited the horror and indignation of the public without the slightest interference on the part of the police. The only case in which any members of the Commission came into disagreeable proximity with the officers of the Criminal Investigation Department was very significant of the ease with which an instrument devised for the protection of the innocent can be converted into a weapon fashioned ready to the hand of the evil-doer.

One of our trusted agents brought us word that a little German girl of delicate health, about 16 years of age, who had been brought over from Cologne by a fraudulent agency, had just been launched upon the streets. She was said to be in the clutches of a bully who lived upon her earnings. She was, we were told, deeply distressed at the necessity which drove her to lead such a life, and we determined at once to rescue her if possible from, the clutches of the man who had imported her in order to profit by her ruin. A French procuress in one of the courts, leading out of Leicester-square undertook to arrange a meeting between the little German girl and myself, presumably, of course, for an immoral purpose, because if we had avowed our real intention we should never have set eyes upon the girl. Punctually at the time appointed the girl was brought to the house of assignation, but as it was impossible to arrange for her rescue under the eyes of the procuress an excuse was made for taking her away to a restaurant. The unfortunate young girl, who could only speak German, told a piteous tale. She was alone in the world, was penniless in London, was suffering from consumption, and not likely to live more than two months. She said that she had been three days without food or lodging before she fell, and her story confirmed our desire to save her.

From the restaurant we took her to a place leading off the Strand, and awaited the arrival of an excellent Swiss lady, who had arranged to take the girl, if she was willing, to a comfortable home. When after some delay this lady arrived, the girl refused to go with her that day. She might call to-morrow, and would bring her box on Saturday, but go home that night she must, for she had her rent to pay. So handing over the sovereign which was to have been her fee, we let her go. On returning home the girl appears to have spoken of the attempt to get her into a home, and the bully who lived upon her gains determined to frustrate our designs. And what did he do? He seems to have gone straight to the police and there laid an information against us imputing all manner of attempts upon the virtue, liberty, and even the life of "an innocent little English girl"–who, as it turned out, was then, and is to this day, a German prostitute walking the Strand. The consequence was that the next night, when two members of our Commission met again at the same place, they were startled by the appearance of a detective, and this is what passed:–

The detective took a seat in the room, and confronted my friend. "Who are you?" he was asked. In answer, he produced his card, similar to a railway season ticket, inscribed with his name. "I am Detective-Sergeant—, of the – Division, I have been sent here to elucidate a case." So saying, he produced a roll of thin foolscap, numbering, perhaps, six or seven closely written sheets. He was requested to tell us what he wanted, and read from his blue foolscap, addressing himself to my friend, who was sitting on the sofa. I do not pretend to give more than the gist of what he read. He informed us that an old gentleman came here and made an agreement (or a young girl to be sold to him. It was agreed that a certain young English girl should pretend to be modest. "English girl," interrupted my companion, "you know she is a little German prostitute now walking the Strand." "Well," said he, "the little German prostitute and the old gentleman met. He seemed to approve after a talk with her, and he was sufficiently satisfied with his bargain to take her to Gatti's to dinner. They dined together there, and then she was taken to a house in a street leading off the Strand. She was taken by the old gentleman into this house, where no questions were asked, led upstairs, where she found another man. The two tried to persuade her to take a situation, offered her drugged coffee and sweets, none of which she would take, and talked to her for a long time, always endeavouring to persuade her to leave London. Presently a woman came in under the guise of the habit of a Sister of Mercy. This lady then talked to the girl, and gave her a Bible, which she tore to pieces, and tried every art to prevail upon her to accede to the request of the two gentlemen in the room. But it was all in vain. The girl saw the fiendish design of the disguised nun, and was eventually allowed to go, having received a douceur for her trouble." This, so far as I remember, was the gist of what the sergeant read. He then began to cross-examine my friend. "You need not inculpate yourself, of course, by answering any of my questions; but I should be obliged if you would tell me all you know. What did you want with the girl, and why did you wish to entice her away?" I thought it best to tell the detective nothing, indeed to try him to the end of his tether by an insolent demeanour and a steady refusal to aid him or the police in any way. "Would you allow us to consult in private for five minutes?" I asked. "Certainly; I will retire." We then agreed to give up my own name with an address where I could be found, and my address only. The sergeant seemed surprised, as I was not mentioned in the statement he read. "That is my name and my address. We refuse to tell you anything. My friend declines to give you either his name and address. Now do what you can. Take us in charge if you like; we should like nothing better." " That is final. You will give me no more information, then?" "No." Having taken the name and address of the willing — , Sergeant — departed, no wiser than he came, and evidently fancying we were a pair of scoundrels. No blame to him. I should like to say a word for his politeness and civility under trying circumstances, for we purposely tried his temper to the utmost. Giving him time to get out, I followed him to see if he could stand the test of a bribe. I found him in the court talking to the servant. "Are you going off to report to Mr. Dunlop?" I asked. "Never mind what I am going to do. I am sorry I cannot introduce you to him to-night in his official capacity." "I have already the pleasure of the superintendent's acquaintance." "I dare say," was the sardonic reply. "May I walk with you a little way?" "If you please. Are you going to tell me what your fnend wanted with the little girl ?" "Certainly not, you must find out for yourself. But supposing I had come out to offer you a ten-pound note to say nothing more." "Now don't you try that game, please, you've got the wrong man." And the sergeant walked off.

Since then we have heard absolutely nothing more of the case, and we have much pleasure in stating that the conduct of Detective — . was perfect throughout.

THEATRES AND EMPORIUMS

A good deal has been said in the course of these articles and in the comments based upon the revelations already made as to the responsibility of the dissolute rich for the ruin of the daughters of the poor. No mistake would be greater, however, than the assumption that those answerable for the wide-spread corruption of the working women of London are solely to be found among the very wealthy and the immoral idlers of the "upper ten." Their share, no doubt, is great, and greater is their responsibility for the abuse of privileges granted them for vastly different ends. If, however, I were asked to describe as by far the most ruinous form of London vice, I would point, not to fashionable West-end houses, such as that kept by Mrs. Jeffries, nor to the systematized business of procuration, but rather to certain of the great drapery and millinery establishments of the metropolis, in which every year hundreds, if not thousands, of young women are ruined. It is not my purpose to give names, and I have no wish to do more at present than indicate one of the most deadly plague spots on the social system. It is pitiful to think of the number of young girls who have been tenderly trained and carefully educated at home and at school in our country villages who will come up to town in the course of the present year only to discover that the business on which their parents fondly built high hopes as to their future position in life is little better than an open doorway—a pathway leading to the hell.

It is said that at a certain notorious theatre no girl ever kept her virtue more than three months; and that at an equally notorious business establishment in West London it is rare to find a girl who has not lost her virtue in less than six months. This may be an exaggeration, of course. Some theatrical managers are, rightly or wrongly, accused of insisting upon a claim to ruin actresses whom they allow to appear on their boards; and it is to be feared that a certain persistent report is not ill founded, and that the head of a great London emporium regards the women in his employ in much the same aspect as the Sultan of Turkey regards the inmates of his seraglio, the master of the establishment selecting for himself the prettiest girls in the shop. Such an example is naturally followed throughout the whole warehouse, from top to bottom. I have not been able to devote much time to the verification of individual cases, but sufficient has come to my knowledge to justify the assertion that while many houses of business employing hundreds of women may be and are excellently conducted, others are little better than horrible antechambers to the brothel. But upon that subject I will not dwell. In Paris, of course, in many houses it is quite understood that girls accept situations not so much for the salary, which is insufficient often to pay their lodgings, as for the opportunities which they furnish for supplementing legitimate earnings by the wages of sin. A similar system is creeping into some fashionable shops in London, and when once it obtains a firm bold the mischief is almost irremediable.

EMPLOYMENT AGENCIES AND SERVANTS' REGISTRIES

It is bad enough when a man kills a sheep for the sake of its fleece, but it would be worse if the animal were slaughtered solely for its ears. This is, however, a fair analogy to the case when girls are ruined not for the sake of the possession of the victim, but solely because an intermediary can turn a miserable commission by luring them into a position from which a life of vice is the only exit. In the course of this inquiry it has come repeatedly under our notice that while many respectable agencies are carried on, even the most respectable are liable to be abused for vicious purposes by unscrupulous men and their female agents, and in some cases there is a suspicion, almost amounting to a certainty, that the agency itself is little better than an organization for carrying on the business of procuration. When you find that a notorious keeper of immoral houses occasionally opens a servants' registry in the intervals when the police have chased her from the pursuit of her ordinary calling, such suspicion is natural, and, unfortunately, it is too often the case that persons engaged in a business which should be beyond reproach have a record more or less immoral, if not, as in some cases, actually criminal. A sojourn in prison for a felony is hardly a better preparation for the honest conduct of an employment agency than the keeping of a disorderly house.

Some of the most scandalous of these agencies are among those which are reputedly the most respectable. Girls are brought from a distance, often from abroad, by promises of a situation which does not exist. They pay their fee and live in continually increasing anxiety either in lodgings connected with the agency or elsewhere until their little capital is exhausted. Debt is incurred, against which their box is held as security, and when all hope disappears the agent who tempted them to London with fair promises of honest and profitable employment suggests that the only mode of making a livelihood is to accept their kind service in introducing them to gentlemen or to keepers of houses who are on the constant look out for respectable young girls. Only this week one of the most widely-known governess agencies in London offered me the choice of several poor girls, speaking French and German, to accompany me as an intimate–too intimate–travelling companion on the Continent There was no disguise whatever about the purpose for which the girl was wanted. She had to be young, not more than twenty-two, pretty, lively, and of full figure, and willing to travel alone with a gentleman, The number of girls whom this firm is said to have been the means of launching upon the London streets who would otherwise have lived quietly at home in Belgium, France, Germany, and Switzerland is I am assured if competent authorities almost incalculable. Other governess agencies will occasionally do the same thing. They get their profit, and for them that is sufficient.

THE IMPORT OF FOREIGN GIRLS TO LONDON

London, say those who are engaged in the white slave trade, is the greatest market of human flesh in the whole world. Like other markets the traffic consists of imports and exports, and although we have heard a great deal of late about the exportation of English girls abroad, there is a chapter quite as ghastly which remains to be written concerning the import of foreign girls into England. The difference between the two is that in England vice is free, whereas on the Continent it is a legalized slavery, and that of course is immense. But so far as the ruin of innocent girls is concerned the compulsion of poverty and helplessness arising from youth, inexperience, friendlessness, and absolute ignorance of the language, is quite as tyrannical as the savagery of the State brothel-keeper and the unfeeling barbarity of the official doctor. Girls are regularly brought over to London from France, Belgium, Germany, and Switzerland for the purpose of being ruined. The idea of the men who import these girls, many of whom are perfectly respectable, is to force them to lead a life of vice from which they can reap a heavy profit. There is a great colony of maquereaux in the French quarter whose chief idea of securing an easy livelihood is to get a girl into their possession, body and soul, to drive her upon the street, and to live and thrive upon the profits of her prostitution.

Some very remarkable cases of importation have been exposed by Miss Sterling, the devoted and public-spirited founder of the Edinburgh and Leith Children's Aid and Refuge. According to the official correspondent, George N——, described by the pastor in Hamburg as "the young German workman who did certainly trade in young girls," got two girls, Annie and Elise, by the following advertisement in the Reform of Hamburg: "A good family in Edinburgh, in Scotland, wish to adopt a girl, age nine to twelve years of age; a child of poor parents or orphan preferred; address letters to No. 424, Stockbridge Post Office, Edinburgh." After Miss Sterling rescued these poor children from his clutches, N—— became very violent, and police protection was afforded Miss Sterling for five months. She was threatened with death, and went about in fear of her life, her only offence being that she had rescued two wee bairns from the hand of a slave trader. It is apparently an organized trade. Much surprise was expressed by the Hamburg Burgomaster that English law did not deal with such cases, and as late as March 8, 1884, Count M�nster referred in terms of honor to the shocking trade which George N—— and others seem to have been carrying on for some time. The stewardesses on Currie's steamers are apparently useful in detecting these offences. The hint ought not to be lost here.

Several times in the course of the present inquiry we have heard of cases, apparently authentic, in which girls who had been struggling vainly for weeks against the necessity of seeking a livelihood on the trottoir had succumbed in some cases only a week, and in others only a day before we heard of the case. One very painful instance of this nature will never be forgotten by those engaged in this inquiry. A German girl who had been brought over by prormises of a situation, and then had found herself confronted by the alternative of starvation or prostitution, was actually brought to the house of a trustworthy person in order to be placed by us in a place of safety. Some misunderstanding arose about the time when we should have arrived, and the girl, timid and mistrustful, took alarm at the arrival of some well-known slave traders of the colony, left the house, and was immediately carried off by the maquereaux, who was furious at the thought that his prey might escape him. The poor girl cast an appealing look to her friend as she was hurried off, but it was of no avail. "It is high time you were doing something," said her captor. "You must start at once." That night she was compelled to receive two visitors, and then she disappeared, as so many others have done, into the great gulf. No traces of her have we been able again to discover, in spite of all efforts. During the operations of the Commission we constantly felt ourselves to be in the position of spectators who watch a shipwreck with straining eyes, making such endeavours as they can to snatch here and there one stray swimmer from a watery grave. A rope is thrown into the abyss; it falls a yard short, and the last chance is gone. The waters close over the strong swimmer in his agony, and no second opportunity is afforded. Occasionally we were more fortunate–not indeed in preventing but in rescuing; and in the case of one victim of this cruellest of all frauds, we took down the following story from her own lips:– HOW MARGUERITE WAS RUINED

Marguerite de S——, a French girl, twenty-one years of age, formerly a leading dressmaker in a Parisian establishment, whose mother is dead, and whose father is foreman in a large French warehouse–a person of much refinement, quick intelligence, and pleasing manners.––was induced to come to this country by an advertisement inserted in the Journal des Renseignements, published by Mdme Pilus, 56, Rue de Richelieu, Paris. This This advertisement offered a nursery governess's place in England to a respectable French girl, and answers were were to be addressed to "M.B ——, 33 —— street, Lambeth London." M. B— professed himself to be the head of an employment agency, for the respectability of which Mdme Palus (sic) vouched "You can put yourself safely in his hands," she said. Now, this M.B —— disreputable even amongt the shadiest characters in the French colony.

He lives in a room for which he pays 3s. 6d. a week rent, and the furniture of his chamber could probably be purchased for 15s. Marguerite wrote to M. B——, applying for the situation, and was forwarded a letter in French, purporting to come from a "Mr. Southern, of Oaley-street, London," who promised that if she came he would "treat her as one of the family." This letter was written by a man whom I have seen, who confesses that he was employed to invent the whole story. There was no "Mr. Southern" in existence, and when she arrived in London upon the day agreed upon, the poor girl made a long and trying search for him in vain. She then betook herself to M. B——'s room to seek explanations. The man whom M.B— employed as his secretary here met her in a state of intoxication, and in escorting her (as he insisted upon doing) to the London Bridge Hotel, where she had previously taken a room, he made improper proposals to her which she indignantly rejected. This the man admits. The next morning M. B——, whom Marguerite describes as "an exceedingly ill-looking man," visited her. Telling her she "arrived too late, the vacancy having been filled up"–she arrived at the time appointed– M. B—— offered to find her another place in three days if she would give him 10s., and she gave him 7s., the only English money she had. In the evening he returned to tell her he hoped to get her a situation, but he feared she was too good-looking for it, as the lady was of a jealous disposition. Claiming that he had been spending money in her interests, he got another 2s. On two following days he came with similar stories with the same result, and at the end of a week she found her small stock of cash had almost disappeared.

I felt myself (she says) utterly helpless, and knowing no other person in London I even clung for guidance and help to M. B—, whose words and behaviour did not inspire me with more confidence than his looks. He advised me to leave the hotel, and offered to find me a cheap apartment. I accepted his offer, and removed to a room at 6s. a week at 19, Manners-street, button-street. Afterwards advertisements appeared on my behalf. There were a few answers, which B— gave me to understand were of a trivial or of an immoral character. On my remarking to B— that I should soon be without money, he said: "You have a nice gold watch and chain; but if you want to get a good advance on them, you must pledge them through me." A day or two before this he tried to get some more money from me. On my refusing, he presently informed me that he was about to leave for Paris for a short trip, as he wanted to find out why Mdme. Pilus kept sending him girls while he had no vacancies open for them. Before taking leave of me he said he would as a dernier devoir introduce me to the Misses Oppenheim, of Berners-street, as he had every confidence that those ladies could shortly procure me a nice place. He took me to their office, and they undertook to find a place for me, but the only situation they ever offered me was that of a nursemaid. This 1 declined and never called on them again. B—left for Paris. After being about a month in London I was visited at my room by a person I had not before met, L—, who I afterwards learned was really in league with B—. I had the day before pledged my gold watch and chain, but having paid my landlady and bought some necessaries, I had spent my money, and really did not know what to do, as I did not like to let my father know how I was situated. I was, therefore, glad to see a person who professed the most friendly intentions in my behalf, as did this L—. He assured me that B— and C— M— had plotted to rob me of my box on my arrival at Victoria station, as it was there that they expected me. He said B— had left in the parcels office a parcel containing nothing more valuable than old newspapers, and it was arranged that when I deposited my box in that office, C— M—should hand to me the ticket given out for this parcel of newspapers, instead of the one for my box. Then L—declared to me that I was in the hands of rogues, that there were three of them, and that they were still conspiring to cheat, rob, and ruin me. You must get out of this house at once," he said, "for if you remain another day B—will contrive to steal your box." I was greatly alarmed at hearing all this. He represented himself as an honest man, and I took him for such. He asked me to go out and breakfast with him, and I consenting, he took me to a neighbouring restaurant. During the meal he assured me that I was a nice little woman, and that he should like to have one just like me. He said he was a merchant, and could earn £5. He offered to take an apartment for me, more suitable than the one 1 was in. He said he would take me to his own apartments, which were in a house kept by a married couple, but he took me instead to apartments in a house kept by a maquereau and his woman, in Poland-street. As soon as I had taken possession of these apartments he unmasked himself, telling me I should have to pay £2 a week for the lodgings, ,£1 5s, for my board, and £1 5s. for his own board, Altogether ,£4 10s. I asked him how 1 was to find the money? "Oh," he said, "of course you must see gentlemen." When I indignantly refused to prostitute myself in order to keep him, he gave me a severe beating. He struck me on the neck and on the head. I shrieked and he left the room, which was ever afterwards closed against him. The maquereau and his woman took my part. But I had brought my box and all my things to their house; I had no money, and there was only one way of paying my way and of saving my things. The lady of the house said she could introduce me to a nice gentleman, who would pay me well. I saw there was no other way of extricating myself from my difficulties, so I consented, and I fell. After staying one week at this place I removed to 142, S—street, where I stayed a fortnight, and then to 129, in the same street, which was kept by the same proprietor. 1 stayed at this last place four months, paying only 27s. 6d. a week. 1 then removed to 156, W—street, Pimlico, where I was staying when I was rescued.

One of our Commissioners interviewed B——, and he not only acknowledged the frauds which he has committed in bringing French girls over, but he also offered to bring over a French girl for our Commissioner provided we advanced 10s. for the preliminary expenses and paid him £5 on delivery of the parcel. His method was to advertise in a Normandy family newspaper, promising excellent situations to be procured through his agency. This man is still at work.

THE FOREIGN EXPORT TRADE

There is not much need to say much about the foreign traffic in English girls, thanks to the labours of Mr. Scott's committee, and the admirable report of Mr. Snagge, which Sir W, Harcourt seems to have forgotten, beyond this–it is the supreme development, the superlative and climax of the possibilities of blank and irremediable temporal damnation which a girl inherits who allows herself to be seduced. Prostitution in England is Purgatory; under the State regulated system which prevails abroad it is Hell. The foreign traffic is the indefinite prolongation of the labyrinth of modern Babylon, with absolute and utter hopelessness of any redemption. When a girl steps over the fatal brink she is at once regarded as fair game for the slave trader who collects his human "parcels " in the great central mart of London for transmission to the uttermost ends o the earth. They move from stage to stage, from town to town–bought exchanged, sold–driven on and ever on like the restless ghosts of the damned, until at last they too sleep "where the wicked cease from troubling and the weary are at rest."

RECRUITS IN THE PROVINCES

If any say that the foreign traffic has ceased, they deceive themselves. Only last week a sample lot of three "coils," or parcels, left the region of Leicester-square for Belgium. Two of them are now in Antwerp, one in Brussels. A much larger consignment is expected shortly. The bagmen of this international traffic are now in the provinces. They say that the London girls have been frightened by the recent exposure of what comes of going abroad. They got three with difficulty. In the provinces they will pick them up more easily. In London they could only get three; in the country they hope to get three dozen. They are recruiting now. The next consignment may start to-morrow night, but of that I have not yet positive information.

The work of inquiring into the ramifications of this new slave trade was the most dangerous part of the investigations. The traffic is almost entirely in the hands of ex-convicts, who know too well the discomforts of the maison correctionelle to stick at any trifles which might remove an inconvenient witness or help them to escape conviction. It was at first a new sensation for me to sit smoking and drinking with men fresh from gaol in the "snug" of a gin palace, and asking as to the precise cost of disposing of girls in foreign brothels. One excellent trader who dwells in such odour of sanctity as can come from having his headquarters within archiepiscopal shade kindly undertook to dispose of a mistress of whom it was supposed that I wished to rid myself before my approaching marriage by depositing her without any ado in a house of ill-fame in Brussels. For this considerable service he would only charge £10. Another agent eagerly competed for the job, and was ready to put it through straight if the other had held back. With a heroism and self-sacrifice worthy of the sainted martyrs a pure and noble girl volunteered to face the frightful risks of being placed in the Belgian brothel if it was thought necessary to complete the exposure. "God has been with me hitherto," said she: "why should He forsake me if in His cause I face the risks? Surely He will take care of me there as well as here." I would not sanction so terrible an experiment. But that there are women capable of such sublimity of devotion to the cause of their outraged and degraded sisters tends to relieve, as by a ray of Heaven's light, the darkness of this awful hell.

AN INTERVIEW WITH AN EX-SLAVE TRADER

This week I had a long interview with John, the S——, who had within the last few weeks returned to London from a prolonged–involuntary–sojourn in his native Belgium. This worthy has long had a high reputation among the exporters of English girls, not only because of his own exploits, but still more because of those of his wife, an Irishwoman, who is now practising as procuress for foreign brothels in the city of Manchester. In April, 1881, John, the S—, was convicted in the Belgian courts of felony and excitement to debauchery, and condemned to six years' imprisonment in the Maison Correctionnelle at Ghent. He was released last April, one year of his sentence being remitted for good behaviour. John is a man who, if well fed and cared for, would be of remarkable, and even commanding, presence. Now he is somewhat broken down, but his countenance is striking, and his grey hair gives him an interesting appearance. We met in a restaurant in the Strand, where we had a long and confidential conversation upon the trade in English girls–a profession which he declares he has now for ever abjured. He has had too much plank bed and bread and water, he says, and having reformed he had no objection to talk very freely concerning the business of exportation.

To what extent," I asked, "do you think English girls leave this country for foreign houses of prostitution?"

John did not reply offhand. He began an elaborate calculation as to the numbers of brothels in Brussels, Antwerp, Lille, Boulogne, and Ostend in which, to his own knowledge, English girls had been placed. Alter a while he said: "I can only speak for Belgium and the North of France. I know nothing of the supply to Bordeaux, Paris, Holland, and the rest of the Continent. But I should think that, on an average, to these places which 1 have named twenty English girls are in the habit of going every month."

That is about 250 par annual, a large figure. How many of these are prostitutes before they start ?"

About one in three, I should think. Two-thirds of them think they are going to situations, and only learn their fate when they are safely within the brothel. Even then the truth is broken to them by degrees. The English girl is placed alone in the midst of foreign women, who are carefully tutored not to excite her suspicions until she is broken in. Then, little by little, she is allowed to see where she is, and she comes to accept her fate as inevitable, and submits."

Don't you think an export of 250 girls per annum is rather large when you take into account the small area which they supply?"

"No," said he; "I think not. Girls do not as a rule stay very long in one house. They are constantly being exchanged and passed on from brothel to brothel, so that there is no knowing how far into the interior of the Continent they may ultimately make their way. They begin in Belgium and the North of France, and are worked gradually inland."

"How many English girls do you regard as the ordinary complement of the houses which you used to supply? "

"One or two is the ordinary rate. I should say that the normal number of English girls in Brussels is twenty to thirty. In Antwerp they are much more numerous. I should say that you would find little difficulty in finding four or five English girls in twenty houses in Antwerp. Possibly there are altogether a hundred English girls in Belgian houses of ill fame at this moment. That of course is more or less of a guess on my part. I have no statistics, but that is what I should expect from what I know of the houses and their habits."

"How are these houses supplied?"

"It is a regular business. I was only in it in a small way. In fact, I only took abroad eleven girls in all, not including those which my wife sent. Of these I took five to Brussels, three to Antwerp, two to Boulogne, and one to Lille. But my experience is a fair sample of the larger traders'. I was paid so much a girl by the keeper of the house, provided that on arrival she passed her examination as a healthy subject. If she was diseased and had to be sent into the hospital I lost my money. The keepers used to promise that if they came out cured, and entered their houses, they would pay me my commission; but they never did," said he, with a sigh over the dishonesty of the keepers.

"What was the usual commission?"

"I have had as much as £10 (250f.), but out of that I had to pay expenses of collection and delivery."

"Are these heavy?"

"Oh, no," said he, "railway and steamboat fare and a few expenses. My wife would go out into the street, and pick up girls— they might either be prostitutes anxious for a change, servant girls out of work, or shop girls. I always told them where they were going to, but others I dare say were less particular. It is very simple. You get the girl to listen to you, and you can persuade her to anything. If they were not as silly as they are, they would never believe you. But they swallow anything. You tell them they will have good situations, fine clothes, liberty to go to the theatre, high wages, and all the inducements which would enable a sharp girl to smell a rat. But they are not sharp girls; they swallow the bait like gudgeons, and off they go."

"How do they go?"

"By Dover to Ostend for the most part. Sometimes the woman of the house comes to Dover to receive them. She takes good care of them after she gets hold of them."

"What are the difficulties in the way of the trade?" "(1.) The possibility that some stewardess or Englishwoman on board the Ostend steamer may get into conversation with the girls, and warn them where they are being taken. If girls get to know that on board, the consignee would be aghast, and the parcel would never reach its destination. (2.) If they are safely landed without having their suspicions aroused, there is a danger that they may take alarm alter they land, when they could make it very disagreeable for us if they communicates with the police. The Belgian police would always befriend the girls, but then, you see, the police speak no English, the girls no French. The interpreting is usually carried on by the keeper, and she takes good care to make the most of her advantage. (3.) After the girls are delivered at their destination they may be got out if any friend appeals to the Procureur du Roi. The English Consuls are not much good. But the Procureur du Roi is bound by law to release any English girl detained in a brothel against her will, even if she has not paid her debt."

"Why, then, do girls remain?"

"They cannot easily summon the Procureur, and then when the opportunity occurs it is so easy to deceive a girl, to make her drunk, or otherwise to spoil her chance of escape. Sometimes girls complain very bitterly, especially at the official surgical inspection. English girls do not like that, and there have been cases where they have resisted it violently. You see in England girls are so free. Belgium is not so free as England, but it is better than France. In the French provincial brothels there is very little liberty. Girls are constantly being changed. Sometimes one girl will be in three or four houses in one year."

"Who are the chief exporters now?"

"F—— has gone to Liverpool, a fine field for picking up girls. My wife is in Manchester, Alfred of the beautiful teeth and some half-dozen others are in London. K——, P——, C——, C——, and R——, all Belgians, are all in the business. The export of little girls of thirteen or fourteen for Continental brothels is chiefly in the hands of a woman named Kate. I do not know who supplies the infants of eight and nine. Most of these agents will place any girl entrusted to them in a foreign brothel, but I—no, not for a thousand pounds! If you want to stop the trade, place a trustworthy person on board steamer to warn the girls, and get some one to see to it that the Procureur du Roi does his duty. That would cut the trade up by the roots so far as it is carried on in unwilling girls."

AN INTERVIEW WITH "A PARCEL" SHIPPED TO BORDEAUX

The following is the story of one who, for no lofty motive but from the dire compulsion of adverse destiny, was doomed for three years and nine months to sojourn in a foreign brothel. This person had spent nearly four years in a house of ill-fame" in Bordeaux, where she had been placed by a scoundrelly Greek who once kept a cigar shop in a street leading off Regent-street, and who took her and three others over from London on the assurance that he would find them good situations either as barmaids or in gentlemen's families. Her story, which is confirmed in many details by her husband, whom she rejoined after her prolonged sojourn in the south of France, is fairly typical of the way in which the foreign slave trade is worked:–

It is now nearly six years since (said Mrs. M—), after my husband's prolonged ill health had brought our little household to the verge of destitution that I left him to make my living. One of my friends, an English girl in an honest situation, told me that a certain Greek, whose address she mentioned, was anxious to take her and other three girls to Bordeaux, where he could find them excellent situations as soon as they arrived. I was unhappy owing to the quarrel with my husband, and I grasped the suggestion that I should go with her to Bordeaux as affording the means of escaping from the associations and sufferings with which I was so painfully familiar in London. I saw the Greek, and he convinced me that he was quite able to fulfil his promise and place me. In a good situation if I would only put myself in his hands. Foolishly enough, for 1 had not learned wisdom by painful experience, I consented to go with my friend and two others. Our names were Mary Hanson, aged twenty, Rosina Marks, whose age I don't remember, Anna Giffard, a dressmaker, aged twenty-five, and myself, Amelia M—, but I went by the name of Amelia Powell. We were all taken down lo St. Katharine's Dock, and placed on board a steamer bound for Bordeaux. We left London on a Thursday night in February or or March of 1879, and arrived in Bordeaux on Sunday, about seven in the evening. From the steamer we were taken direct, suspecting nothing, to the house of Mdme. Suchon, 36, Rue Lambert, which we believed to be an hotel, or the house of the friend to whom the Greek was about to introduce us; but the landlady was very kind, and we felt convinced that the Greek was a man of his word. On Monday, however, a cruel awakening awaited us. Our own clothes were taken away, and we were tricked out with silk dresses and other finery. Before that, however, we were taken to a doctor. We were alarmed at this, and protested, but unfortunately we could speak no French, and the doctor was almost as ignorant of English. What were we to do? We were alone in a strange land; the man who had taken us over had disappeared. We were absolutely at the mercy of the keepers of the house. After the examination the mistress gave us the fine clothes I have spoken of, and insisted that very night, after giving us champagne, upon introducing us to gentlemen. I objected, and declared that I should leave. "You can't do that," said the landlady, "because you are indebted to me eighteen hundred francs." "Eighteen hundred francs?" said I. "Why, I have not been in the house two days." "Oh, you forget," said she ; "you have to pay the cost of your commission for being brought over, and the price of the silk dress you are wearing." That is the regular rule, as I afterwards learned. Girls are brought from England under the belief that they are going to a pleasant situation, and then they are consigned to one of the houses at so many pounds per head. This purchase-money or commission, which varies from £10 upward, is entered against the girl as a debt to her landlady. That, however, is not the worst. They equip you in fine clothes, which they insist upon you taking, and then debit you with twice their value, running up in this way a debt of perhaps 1,800 f. I was told that I must be a good girl, and do as they wished me to, and I would soon earn sufficient money to get back to my husband, but if I did not I would never see him again. I may mention that I told the doctor that I was a married woman. "Where is your husband?" he said, and proceeded without further notice with my examination. It was some time before I could reconcile myself to receiving gentlemen, but what weighed with me was that unless I consented I should never earn sufficient money to pay off my debt and return to London. In order to raise funds I was submissive, and being then young and attractive I earned my money in less than six months. Of course none of that money actually remains with you. It is entered to your credit in the books of the establishment, and the theory is that when you have worked off your debt you are free to go, but the keeper takes very good care that you shall never work off your debt. When the account shows that you have only four or five hundred francs against you the mistress sets to work to induce you, by cozening, cajoling, or absolute fraud, to accept other articles of clothing. Thus you go on month after month. "How long did you stay there?" "Three years and nine months." "And why in the world did you not communicate with your husband?" "We were never allowed to send letters out of the house. Letters were allowed to come in after they had been read by the mistress, but no replies were ever permitted. Sometimes we used to try and send messages by English sailors who used to visit us, but never any answer came. There were seventeen girls in the house, which was a large one, the entry being three francs. Ours was a middle-class house as distinguished from the low class one, the entrance to which is one franc, and the fashionable house in Rue Berguin, where the entrance fee is ten francs and only four girls are kept. When I was there an English girl called S—, who was said to be the daughter of a coach-builder in the Edgware-road, died. A sum stood on the book as due to the house, and when a brother came over from London to take her dead body home for burial, the mistress refused to allow the corpse to be removed until the debt was paid. She had been taken from England to Spain and had been bought or exchanged from the Spanish house to the one in Bordeaux where she died. One of the English girls who came out with me–Mary Hanson–was sold off to South America. When I say sold I mean that an agent who was picking up girls arranged to pay her debt, and took her off with him to the new world. She assented, as girls always do when they have been long in one house, and see no prospect of paying their debt, for those who want to remove them always hold out inducements that they will be able to buy their liberty much sooner in the new place to which they are going." "Do you know any girls who have ever bought their liberty?" "No. We are always trying and trying, but we never succeed, although we have earned sufficient money over and over again to pay for all that has been spent upon us, but every artifice is used by the keepers, as I have explained, to hold us in their power. Drink is a potent agency and easily used." "How many English girls were there in the house of Mdme. Suchon? Two; but we used to meet with others who were in other houses in the town at the visite when we went to see the doctor at the public building in the Rue Graffe on Tuesdays, Thursdays, and Saturdays. Mary Hanson came round to bid us good-bye before she went to South America." "Could she not have made her escape when visiting?" "She was not alone. We were never allowed out except in company with the mistress." "How was it, then, that you got free?" "A gentleman from Toulouse took a fancy to me, paid off all my debts, and gave me money to pay my passage to London. Otherwise I should have been thereto this day." "What English girl did you leave in the house?" "Poor Rosina Marks, who cried very piteously when I came away." 'How lucky you are, Amelia,' she said; 'as for me, I shall never be able to pay my debt, and shall die here.'" "Is Rosina there still?" "To the best of my belief, but of course she is never allowed to write, and all that I know is that she was there two years ago, and I have never heard of her death. Her family were publicans in Southampton, and her father was employed at Squire — near that town. A very timid girl was Rosina, and madame used to bully her fearfully. I have often wished that something could be done to get her out, but there seems no chance."

Some one should try to do something for poor Rosina–if she be still alive and is still at Bordeaux. But who knows? She may be dead, or sold to Spain or elsewhere, or, like many others, she may have drunk away her reason and her senses. There are plenty more going the same road. Every now and then we hear of the mysterious disappearance of girls. Boys, although much more adventurous, do not disappear in this way. The inference is plain. There have been the cases from West Ham, the case of the girl Hearnden, at Folkestone, the case of the granddaughter of a correspondent on the south coast, who has written to us imploring to know whether we can help her to tidings of her vanished child. Now that the silence has been broken we shall hear of many such, and regret their endless multiplication. The one safeguard is publicity, publicity, publicity. And all who attempt to silence the voice of warning must share the guilt of those upon one small portion of whose crimes it is our proud privilege to have turned a little of the wholesome light of day.

Made in the USA
Las Vegas, NV
07 July 2022

51253713R00056